The Glitter Effect

To Suzanne —
Thanks for Reading!

Timothy Lewis

Lana Teegen

ENDORSEMENTS

The Glitter Effect is an action packed book full of adventure and mystery. Each chapter leaves the reader eager to read more.
—**Barbara Bain**, retired elementary school teacher, and inspiration for the "Barbara Bain English Language Arts and Social Studies Model Classroom" at West Texas A&M University

What kids wouldn't love the opportunity to solve a crime! Tim's vivid descriptions and thrill packed prose make this a fun, fast read!
—**Marilyn Childers**, retired elementary school teacher.

I am so happy I got to read *The Glitter Effect*. I liked the mystery of the story. I hope everyone likes reading it as much as I did.
—**Hadley Holt**, age 9

This is a great book. It is a mystery me and my friends would want to solve. Jerry and Hal are amazing. Jerry really reminds me of myself. I would recommend this book to anyone. I hope to read about the adventures of Jerry and Hal in a sequel.
—**Bode Miller**, age 11

Mystery, friendship, and family ... Hal and Jerry will quickly become your new best friends and leave you eagerly awaiting the next case to be solved.

—**Tricia Shaw**, Library Assistant, Canyon, TX Area Library

THE GLITTER EFFECT

TIMOTHY LEWIS

ELK LAKE PUBLISHING INC
PUBLISHING THE POSITIVE
Plymouth, Massachusetts

COPYRIGHT NOTICE

The Glitter Effect

Cover and Interior Design: Lana Ziegler, Derinda Babcock
Editor(s): Linda Harris, Deb Haggerty
PUBLISHED BY: Elk Lake Publishing, Inc., 35 Dogwood Drive, Plymouth, MA 02360, 2021

_____

Library Cataloging Data
Names: Lewis, Timothy (Timothy Lewis)
The Glitter Effect / Timothy Lewis
106 p. 23cm × 15cm (9in × 6 in.)
ISBN-13: 978-1-64949-445-0 (paperback) | 978-1-64949-446-7 (trade paperback) | 978-1-64949-447-4 (e-book)
Key Words: Skateboard mysteries & detective stories; Crime solving best friends; Summer vacation action & adventure; Middle grade mysteries & detective stories; Middle grade religious/Christian fiction; Juvenile mysteries & detective stories; Juvenile religious/Christian fiction
Library of Congress Control Number: 2021950257 Fiction

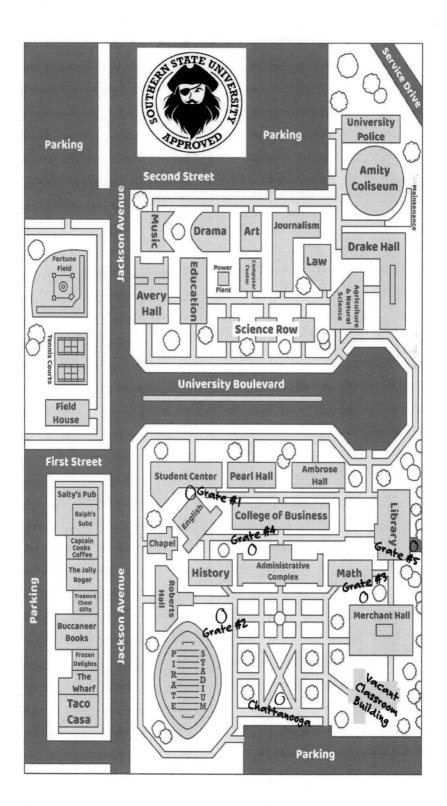

DEDICATION

To America's finest, the men and women who serve in law enforcement and our armed forces. Thank you for your commitment, bravery, honor and sacrifice.

ACKNOWLEDGMENTS

Enormous gratitude to Deb, Linda, Derinda, and the rest of the talented publishing team at Elk Lake. Your combined efforts made my prose shine.

Also, thanks to the bevy of family and friends who offered their time, support and valuable comments.

And to my wife, Dinah, who believed in me long before I believed in myself.

Plus our daughter, Lana, who as a child loved the initial story drafts, then grew up to design the cover.

Finally, praise be to God, the Author of us all.

CHAPTER ONE: POLICE TROUBLE

Whack.

The shiny skateboard flew through midair and slammed into hard concrete. The board teetered on the edge of the middle step, then slid off with a jolting thud.

"Yes." Hal raised his fisted hands in a victory salute. "Hey, Jerry ... watch me do an axle stall on the top step."

"Dude, next funeral's yours." Jerry picked up his board and plopped down on the soft grass to give his friend room. "Gonna be sweet to see you eat cement. Dibs on your board when you die?"

"Funny." Hal rolled his way up the sidewalk into starting position, pivoted, and faced the wide steps. He spent the summer practicing his skateboarding maneuvers, eager to be the best skater in the sixth grade when school began. He chuckled. *What would Jerry do with two boards when he struggles to ride one?*

"And now, ladies and gentlemen," Hal announced toward a vacant building. "The Olympic Skateboarding

Champion, Hal Tanner, will defy the natural law of gravity right before your—"

"I'm hungry." Jerry stood. "Before you smash your brains, let's ride over to the Drag and get something to eat. Don't you want a last meal?"

The Drag, or Jackson Avenue, was a fast-food junkie's dream. Named after former US President, Andrew Jackson, the street bordered the western edge of Southern State University—SSU for short.

"And now, ladies and gentlemen," Hal announced a second time. He lifted his hand toward his future admirers. "The Olympic—"

"I'm still hungry. How 'bout pizza?"

Hal watched his buddy pick up his board. He'd probably grown a whole pant size larger since the end of school. "Can't you go for an hour without wanting something to eat?"

"Sure. Sometimes, I need something to drink too." Jerry mopped sweat from his freckled round face with the stretched-out bottom of his T-shirt. His black shorts drooped several inches past his knees. "Breakfast was two hours ago." He tapped his large smartwatch, the type not paired with a phone.

Hal grimaced.

Jerry loved the watch, which was nothing but an embarrassing clone—a knockoff. He'd ordered the smartwatch from a company going out of business. The manufacturer boasted an alarm database storing hundreds of terrifying sounds. One matched the roar of a jet engine, another the rumble of a powerful earthquake. The only noise Jerry could upload was a crying baby.

Hal clamped his teeth together to keep from hurting his friend's feelings. *Maybe he'll lose the stupid watch, or I'll get lucky and somebody will steal it. Except Jerry would order another one.*

Unlike Hal's parents, Jerry's were rich. They griped about spending money, caved, and allowed their son anything he wanted … most anything.

THE GLITTER EFFECT

The boys sought smartphones because of instant messaging and the cool, new apps.

Jerry's parents held out for a month before letting him order a watch to stop his constant begging.

Hal received a single, emphatic "no", followed by a suppertime lecture on cyber safety and spending money wisely. He argued how the popular kids had smartphones, offering to forfeit his allowance for the next five years.

"Serving God is more important than status." Hal's dad handed his empty plate to his wife.

I do serve him. At least I try. I surrendered my heart to Jesus a couple of years ago at church camp.

"Or wanting material things." His mom took Hal's plate. She announced buttermilk pie for dessert, a signal to drop the subject.

Hal did. Though he considered pressing harder at a future date since persistence landed Jerry a watch.

He glanced at Jerry whose family ate together in front of the television. After a brief, premeal memorized prayer, God wasn't mentioned.

He didn't regret inviting Jerry on this trip to visit his older brother, but the food thing was getting annoying. Hal was proud of Rick, a junior journalism major and editor of the SSU school newspaper.

"Why don't you give Mom and Dad a break and come bug me for a couple of weeks," Rick joked over the phone three weeks earlier. "My roommate's gone second summer session. The apartment's mine."

"Sure." Hal tried not to sound too excited. He and Rick could do fun things again.

"Since I work during the day, invite your forever-hungry friend."

"Jerry?"

"Yeah. The kid eats more than a pro football team. You two can hang around campus while I'm at the office."

"O--kay." He preferred Rick's company, yet spending two weeks at such a cool place would be worth it.

3

"Tell what's-his-name he'd better bring money for food. Uh-oh, another call beeps. Gotta go."

"His name's Jerry ... Jerry Morris," Hal said, but Rick was gone.

Pushing away thoughts of spending time with his older brother, he considered the invitation to bring his best friend. Jerry's love for snacks and chocolate milk had saved Hal from permanently losing both front teeth the summer after fourth grade.

He'd been invited to skateboard with three of the most popular athletes in school. The boys rode to a nearby creek. A kid they didn't know—Jerry—sat atop a dry concrete spillway eating barbequed potato chips and drinking a bottle of chocolate milk. Jerry waved hello, but they ignored him.

When the skaters convinced Hal to ride down the steep spillway first, he crashed into a boulder, knocking out both front teeth. Blood dribbled everywhere. Everyone vanished except Jerry, who calmly dropped Hal's teeth into the remaining milk. "Don't worry, my dad's a dentist. He'll stick 'em back in your mouth."

The milk's calcium saved Hal's teeth. He and Jerry became best friends.

The sudden wail of an approaching siren jarred Hal's thoughts.

Lights flashed.

Tires squealed.

A dark-gray patrol car screeched to a halt on a side street no more than fifty yards from the boys. Climbing out was the same campus cop who'd threatened severe punishment earlier in the week.

"What now?" Jerry wrung out the sweat from the front of his T-shirt. "We stopped riding our skateboards in front of the college library. We did what he told us." Tears puddled in Jerry's eyes.

Hal's stomach dropped down to his toes. He grabbed his board and tried to remain calm, but a million thoughts ricocheted off his brain.

THE GLITTER EFFECT

Run.

Run fast.

Get out of here.

There's something weird about this guy.

Don't take his nonsense.

No.

Don't run.

He's a cop.

Running from cops is stupid.

He must be after somebody else.

"You said *this* building's empty." Jerry's voice trembled. "We could skateboard over here and not bother anybody."

"Right." Hal spun a wheel on his board.

"Wrong. We're probably at another library. Somebody's complained."

"No way." Hal studied the vacant classroom building. "We looked in the windows. There's not a stick of furniture in the whole place." Though Jerry was twelve, he sometimes showed less reasoning ability than Hal's five-year-old sister, Bethany.

"We're gonna go to jail," Jerry whined. "Moldy bread and tap water for the rest of our lives."

"Quiet." Hal spun another wheel. Jerry chose the dumbest times to kid around. At least Hal hoped he was kidding. "Got to be a logical mistake. Officer Bratton is confused."

During the library incident, he'd noticed the cop's badge and memorized his appearance. Overweight. Sloppy. Sweating through his wrinkled blue uniform. A fat cigar clamped between his tobacco-stained teeth.

Hal shuddered as he remembered a line of brown drool oozing from the corner of Bratton's mouth. The disgusting slime dribbled down his chin and hung in the stubble.

"Sick." Hal scrubbed the corner of his mouth. "I wonder if he lights the cigar, or—"

"Chews it." Jerry mimed rolling a cigar around in his mouth.

"Hey." Bratton huffed across the lawn. "You punks are in a restricted area. Freeze."

He took another step and dozens of lawn sprinklers sprang to life.

Miniature geysers shot up everywhere, spurting, and clicking in alternate rhythms.

One hit Bratton under his chin and knocked him off balance. The cop fell face down, grinding his cigar into the wet turf.

Hal tried not to snicker, but the scene mimicked a cartoon.

Bratton raised his head and shouted. "Wiley, you little half-brain joker. I'll get you for this."

A shriek of wild laughter burst from behind a tall cedar hedge next to the vacant building.

Hal caught a glimpse of someone's legs in pale green work pants with shiny black combat boots. From Bratton's reaction, he guessed the cop knew someone named Wiley turned on the water.

Drenched, Bratton sat up. Grass clippings and pine needles matted the front of his shirt. The cigar—still in his mouth—was L-shaped. He attempted to stand, but his right heel skidded on a slick spot of bare earth. This time, he sat hard, splattering mud on his uniform. Dark blobs speckled his face.

The same laughter erupted from behind the hedge.

Bratton wasn't amused. He pushed himself up. Sprays of water continued to slap back and forth across his thick legs. Hatred blazed at Hal and Jerry.

"You two juvenile delinquents must consider yourselves clever." He inched toward the boys. "Thought I wouldn't notice your smart-aleck faces over on the old side of campus."

"No-uh-sir." Hal moved closer to Jerry. "I mean ... we were ...." He was too confused to answer. The whole situation, twisted. *What crime have we committed? Why didn't Bratton chase after this Wiley guy?*

"What's big brother gonna do when I run you two in?" Bratton patted muddy handcuffs. "Bet he'll put the story in the paper. Print real news for a change."

Hal wished he'd never told the cop about his relation to Rick. The last thing Hal needed was his *perfect* brother rescuing him from another screw-up. Word would get back to their parents, who'd demand Hal act ... as responsible as Rick.

An evil grin twitched on Bratton's lips. "Picture the headline. *Hot Shot Editor's Kid Brother Breaks Law.*"

"We stayed away from the library." Hal folded his arms. "We've done nothing wrong."

"Yeah." Jerry matched Hal's stance. "We've done nothing ... wrong ... I hope."

Bratton shoved a stubby finger toward the front door of the vacant building. "See the sign? *Building Closed - Area Off Limits.* Since these steps belong to this building, you've committed a serious violation."

Hal studied the sign. Printed on letter size copy paper, the words weren't centered and too small to read from the steps. "Wasn't there yesterday."

Stooping close, Bratton blew putrid breath into Hal's face. "You're as blind as your pompous brother. Sign's been there for months. You, runts, are coming with me."

The sprinklers halted as a clock tower chimed in lunchtime's joyous rush. Hungry students poured from adjacent classroom buildings and crowded around campus food vendors. Others lounged in cool shade, digging sandwiches and chips from their backpacks. Cars honked friendly hellos. Bicycles and skateboards rolled everywhere.

The lights atop Bratton's patrol car continued to flash. Opening a rear passenger door, he motioned the boys inside. He climbed into the driver's side and gunned the engine.

People stared.

Hal slumped down as low as possible. The protective steel mesh barrier separating the front seat from the back seat squashed against his bare knees.

Jerry sat frozen, his only movement an occasional poke at the buttons on his watch.

Bratton switched on the siren and sped into traffic.

Turned corners on two wheels.

Roared through stop signs.

Cursed whoever was in his way.

Sweat dribbled down Hal's face and neck. The air-conditioner whined, yet he felt no air, making breathing difficult. He pushed the switch to lower the window.

Nothing.

The one to unlock the door ...

Dead.

A single, salty tear followed another. He and Jerry were trapped with no way out. Hal wanted to ask God for help but couldn't find the words.

Bratton slammed on the brakes. "We're here," he growled. "Hope you gentlemen enjoyed the ride."

"Where are we?" Jerry whispered.

Hal wiped his eyes and peered outside.

Reality kicked him in the stomach.

Jail was a better destination.

CHAPTER TWO: THE REWARD

Muddy shoes clomped up two flights of stairs behind Hal and Jerry. A door at the top was painted to duplicate the front page of the university newspaper, *The Cutlass*. The headline read: *Welcome to the Journalism Department— Pride of SSU.*

Bratton shoved the boys aside and burst into the outer office. "Where's Tanner?" Dried bits of mud still clung to his salt and pepper hair. Grass clippings floated to the floor.

The startled receptionist stood. "He's in a meeting." She blocked Tanner's door. "Would you care to leave a message?"

"This is official police business." Bratton tried to wave her aside, but she stood her ground. "I'll find him myself."

The cop grabbed both boys by the backs of their necks, forcing them down a short hallway into a wide room.

Journalism students crowded behind computer screens atop news desks cluttered with fast-food trash and disposable coffee cups. Most workers ate lunch, texting or talking on their phones between bites. Along the far side, a glass wall partitioned a row of private offices.

"Where's the no-good editor?"

The newsroom hushed into an eerie calm.

Keyboards stopped clicking.

Phones beeped silent.

No one spoke.

All eyes focused upon the three intruders.

Hal wanted to shrink to ant size and crawl under the nearest laptop.

The cop's bristly grin matched his taunt. "Hey, Tanner? Found something of yours."

A young man wearing shorts and flip-flops stepped from the middle office. "Bratton. Let go of my little brother."

"*Lieutenant* Bratton to you, Pal. A real newsman would've noticed the gold bars."

Rick looked him up and down. "All I see is mud. Where'd you find puddles to play in during a drought?"

Snickers echoed around the room.

The cop swelled up like a jellyfish. His neck veins bulged. He released the boys to wave his arms and point at them. "Found these two punks messing around the old classroom building. Area's off-limits. Second time this week they've disrupted valuable police work."

Rick shot Hal a stern look. "True?"

Hal wished he could explain in private. He felt like a tennis ball at the US Open, slammed from both sides as the whole world watched.

"Now you listen to me, Tanner." Bratton jabbed both stubby index fingers at Rick. "I've no time to babysit. The chief's working the entire force overtime to solve an important case."

"I'm aware of the missing bikes." Rick hooked his thumbs on his shorts pockets. "Over a hundred vanished off racks in the past three days. Campus police are baffled. No leads."

Bratton threw back his head and hooted. "Shows what you know. Everything's under control."

"I disagree." Rick stepped forward. "Latest FBI stats indicate bike theft is a growing problem nationwide, especially at universities. We'll print a big story in tomorrow's paper. Or you can read it online ... during an idle moment."

"All you college kids are spoiled." Bratton flicked a lump of mud off his shirt. "Come here on your folks' money, dressed for a day at the beach, and play newspaper. Wouldn't know an honest day's work from a wiener roast. I'd ..."

The louder he spoke, the bigger his arm motions grew. He ranted about the commitment involved in police work, a dangerous job with little pay.

During the part about *self-sacrifice*, Hal noticed the stack of bright orange posters. Taking one, he read:

$1000 REWARD.
THROUGH PRIVATE DONATION, A REWARD OF ONE THOUSAND DOLLARS IS OFFERED TO ANYONE WITH INFORMATION LEADING TO THE ARREST OF PERSON(S) INVOLVED IN THE RECENT BICYCLE THEFTS. CALL 223-1587 OR TEXT 223-1588. ALL COMMUNICATION IS KEPT CONFIDENTIAL.

"Give me that." Bratton jerked the poster away from Hal and scanned it. "Was my department notified?"

"For your information, Lieutenant, the scoop about a reward arrived this morning in an email from your boss. I replied immediately. My staff is pleased to print and distribute the posters. We'll also spread the word on social media."

Rick stepped forward. "Chief Nelson and I are an efficient, crime-fighting team, don't you agree?"

Hal thought if the big cop's face became any redder, his head would explode.

Bratton spoke in a deliberate whisper. "We'll see who's the crime fighter, Mister Editor." He wadded up the poster, tossed it at Hal, and stomped out.

Dead silence.

Someone clapped.

Applause exploded across the room.

Hal felt proud and sick at the same time. His older brother had won again.

Rick clapped his hands. "Okay. Fun's over. Everybody back to work. We've got a newspaper to finish." The voices, beeps, and clicks resumed as if releasing the pause feature on a TV movie.

"C'mon," Hal whispered to Jerry. "Let's hurry back and get our boards." Discovering the reward posters was a stroke of pure luck. Hal wanted to leave before his older brother asked any more questions.

"Right. All the hollering made me hungrier. Let's go."

"Not yet." Rick stood behind the boys, his hands on his hips, his voice stern. "You two aren't going anywhere … until we talk."

CHAPTER THREE: BIG BROTHER

Rick led the boys into his office and shut the door.

Hal glanced around. *The space is as organized as his apartment. Everything has a proper place. His room back home was the same way.*

"Have a seat." Rick motioned toward a couple of padded folding chairs positioned in front of his desk.

"The sign wasn't there yesterday," Hal blurted. "We weren't aware the building's off-limits."

"Y-yeah," Jerry added. "Didn't know we'd bothered people in the library either."

"Hush," Hal mouthed. *Sometimes Jerry doesn't have the savvy of a dried-up worm.*

Rick placed his finger in front of his lips to signal quiet. He didn't sit, but moved to a narrow window and peered outside.

Hal stared at his brother.

Jerry fiddled with buttons on his watch.

No one spoke.

Rick's profile reminded Hal of their dad—dark hair and eyes, with a thick muscular build. Hal and Bethany were as slender as their mom, plus inherited her sandy blonde hair and light blue eyes.

More than the silence, Hal was uncomfortable with the journalism awards framed on the wall behind Rick's desk. The collection was akin to the trophies displayed in the family room at home—baseball, debate team, creative writing. Each one belonged to his big brother.

Except one.

A shiny blob Bethany constructed out of Play-Doh and silver glitter. The homemade trophy was a *thank you* to Hal for teaching her to tie her shoes.

Big Deal.

Anyone could tie shoelaces.

Hal decided to study the floor.

"I'm sorry, guys," Rick said, at last, still facing the window. "I'm sorry you're caught in the middle."

Hal's jaw dropped. He couldn't believe what he heard. Why would Rick apologize?

"I never dreamed Bratton would take his anger out on you two. Proves what a low-down snake he is."

"Are you gonna call my dad and mo—"

Hal cupped a hand over Jerry's mouth. "You're sorry we're in the middle of what?"

Rick moved away from the window and sat on the corner of his desk. "Look. Stay away from libraries and vacant buildings. Above all, keep clear of Bratton. He's one badge-heavy cop."

"Badge what?" Hal was unfamiliar with the term.

"Badge-heavy—cops who abuse their authority. They throw their weight around and pick on innocent people. Officer Bratton's irresponsible actions could give our fine police department a bad name."

"So why don't they fire him?" Jerry drew his index finger across his throat.

Hal had never heard his friend ask such an intelligent question.

"I wish change was simple." Rick stood. "Let me show you something."

The boys followed him into the busy newsroom, which now mirrored the steady workings of a high-performance engine.

They stopped in front of a row of short filing cabinets. Rick pulled open a drawer and thumbed through a stack of newspapers. "This process is faster on my laptop." He smiled. "I want you guys to see the hard copy. Here it is. June 21, 2007."

Hal leaned forward to see the paper. "What's an old *Cutlass* got to do with Bratton?"

Rick spread the newspaper on top of the cabinet. "Read the front-page headline."

"**W.F. Bratton Receives Congressional Medal Of Honor,**" Hal read aloud. "You mean Officer Bratton is a hero?"

"Not by a long shot. Keep reading."

> Lieutenant W.F. Bratton, son of Prof. and Mrs. Lawrence Bratton, was awarded the prestigious Congressional Medal Of Honor in a ceremony at the White House on Tuesday. The former SSU law enforcement major earned America's highest honor by saving the lives of four fellow soldiers. Lt. Bratton was deployed to Afghanistan during Operation Enduring Freedom as a member of a U.S. Army Special Forces scouting unit.

Hal wrinkled his forehead. "Sounds like a hero to me. I can't believe he's the same guy."

"Me either," Jerry added.

Rick leaned against the cabinet. "The man in the story *is* a hero, in more ways than one."

"But you said, 'not by a long shot.' I don't understand." Hal hated when he couldn't tell if his brother was teasing.

"Officer Bratton—the police lieutenant—is named Curtis. The army lieutenant who won the medal is his younger brother. The initials W.F. stand for William Frances. However, everyone calls him Wiley. He works here on campus as a groundskeeper.

Hal and Jerry spoke at the same time.

Rick's smile morphed into a chuckle as the boys relayed the incident of the mysterious Wiley and the lawn sprinklers.

Hal laughed until his insides ached.

"Awesome." Rick's laughter upped the merriment. "Wiley, the great practical joker, continues to strike."

Hal enjoyed hearing his older brother laugh, reminiscent of their last backyard campout. They'd stayed up all night telling ghost stories. Acting scared, Rick made a million goofy faces. They laughed hard enough for every outdoor neighborhood dog to howl in response, which made the situation funnier. The next week, Rick left home for college and everything changed.

"You mean they won't get rid of Officer Bratton 'cause his little brother is a hero?"

"Not hardly, Jerry." Rick folded his arms. "The cop remains on duty out of respect to their father. Lawrence Bratton was one of the great presidents of this university."

"When?" Hal imagined a hundred-year-old man with a beard to his knees.

"Twenty-five years ago."

Jerry made an airy whistle. "Pretty far back." He studied his fingers. "Five whole hands."

"What happened to their dad?"

"His wife developed cancer and died several years ago. Shortly after her death, he suffered a heart attack."

"The dude's dead, too?"

Hal glared at his friend.

"He's alive, yet remains in poor health." Rick folded the newspaper. "The strain of Mrs. Bratton's illness, along with Wiley's injury in Afghanistan, was too stressful.

Hal cocked his head to one side. "You mean something bad happened to Wiley?"

Rick stood and dug out another newspaper. "I won an award for this story."

As before, Hal read aloud:

Still A Hero
by Rick Tanner

More than a decade has passed since Lieutenant W.F. (Wiley) Bratton received the coveted Congressional Medal Of Honor. His feat of carrying four wounded soldiers to safety under heavy enemy fire is common knowledge. He is a real-life hero. However, Wiley's heroism didn't stop when calm ensued. Few are aware of the closed head injury he suffered during the lifesaving incident.

Hal stopped reading. "What's a closed head injury?"

Rick thought for a moment. "The wound doesn't break the skin. For lack of the proper technical term, Wiley's brain was bruised."

"Did it hurt?" Jerry rubbed his forehead.

"What do you think?" *A head injury would never happen to Jerry. He doesn't have a brain to bruise.*

Jerry tugged a strand of his topmost hair. "Is Wiley a double hero?"

Rick repositioned the paper. "Listen to this next paragraph.

To most, military conflicts in the fight against global terrorism become distant memories. Not for Wiley. His fight continues—for he must struggle with the result of his injury every day. The enemy? A language disorder called conduction aphasia. Through therapy, Wiley has won major battles. Yet his war with words could last the rest of his life.

"What's conduction aph ...?" Hal couldn't remember the rest.

"*A-fay-zsha.*" Rick looked up from the paper. "An aphasia is when someone's brain sends the wrong instructions to their mouth. They know what they want to say, but can't."

"Okay." Hal shifted in his chair. "What does *conduction* mean?"

"It's the type of aphasia affecting Wiley. Sometimes he speaks pretty close to normal. His brain remembers how to make his mouth form words. At other times his brain forgets, and he makes little sense. The condition's worse when he's tired or upset."

Jerry raised an eyebrow. "I'll bet some people make fun."

Rick nodded. "They don't understand, which is no excuse. However, you two know the truth."

The year 2007 happened before Hal was born. Still, he pictured the brave American soldier who'd dreamed of becoming a cop, and the four soldiers he'd saved—who'd have kids of their own. He thought about sacrifice and how Bratton screamed at Wiley under the sprinklers.

"It's not fair. Wiley studied to be a cop. He'd be the best."

"I know, Hal." Rick slid the newspaper back inside the drawer.

Whaaah! Whaaah! Whaaah! The alarm on Jerry's watch sounded.

Rick jumped. "Who's hiding the baby? That's the loudest cry I've ever heard."

Jerry raised his arm and grinned. "My watch alarm reminds me when it's time to eat—or past time."

Rick wrinkled his forehead. "What about the red button?"

"Push it, and the alarm sounds for a whole minute. Scares off muggers and stuff."

Hal tried to keep from snickering. *Who'd want to mug Jerry?*

"C'mon, Hal." Jerry stood. "I'm starved. Let's head over to the Drag and get a pizza."

Hal glanced at his older brother. He was different, more relaxed, reminding Hal of when they were little. "Wanna come with us?"

"Better not." Rick patted Hal on the shoulder. "I have to work on this bike theft story. Maybe tomorrow." Rick pointed at the stack of orange reward posters. "Need to find someone to hang these posters around campus. Promised Chief Nelson they'd be up today."

"Let us do it." Hal owed Rick for getting them out of the mess with Bratton.

"I don't know ...." Rick strode to a nearby window. "It's a big university. Plus there are the businesses on the drag."

"We'll put one up at the pizza place." Hal grabbed the posters and backed toward the door.

"And the ice cream joint." Jerry licked his lips.

Hal slowed to a stop as Rick turned in his direction. As with their dad, Rick's face bore a half-worried, half-proud expression.

"Okay, if anyone on campus questions you, show them the stamp on the back. Any sign posted on university property must first be approved by Chief Nelson or the Dean of Student Life."

"We'll remember." Hal swung open the door. The boys headed for the stairs.

"Watch out for Bratton," Rick yelled across the newsroom. "He's got you on his radar. I'm sure to receive a nasty phone call."

"Tell him we're working for the chief." Hal's voice echoed in the stairwell.

CHAPTER FOUR: AMAZING DISCOVERY

The boys scrambled down the stairs and out the front doors of the journalism building.

Heat radiated from a cloudless sky, dancing in waves across the tops of parked cars.

"Let's go grab our boards." Hal took off in a jog. "Whoever stole bicycles wouldn't hesitate to grab a couple of unattended skateboards."

"Slow down," Jerry puffed between words. "I can't run on an empty stomach. When are we going to have lunch?"

Hal slowed to a fast walk but didn't answer. Food was the last thing he wanted. A couple of nagging questions played tug of war in the pit of his stomach. If he and Jerry broke the law, why didn't Bratton haul them to the SSU police station? And who posted the *Building Closed* sign? It wasn't there yesterday.

The boys crossed between a row of brick buildings housing biology and chemistry labs. They passed a couple of dorms, and the College of Business. The route through this section of the campus was new to Hal. Pausing to check his bearings, he eyed the top story of the Administrative Complex. The vacant building wasn't far.

"I'm thirsty. Can't we get a drink?" Jerry panted, catching up. "Do you want me to fry from heatstroke?" His face bore a deeper shade of red than his hair. Strands not plastered to his forehead stuck straight up. Globs of facial sweat dripped onto his T-shirt leaving enormous wet spots.

"Okay." Hal sighed and scanned the immediate area. "Let's try the building over there."

An automatic door swung open with a blast of cold, musty air. In an instant, Hal knew where they were. He'd know blindfolded. Every library on the planet smelled like a mixture of dust, hardback encyclopedias, and Elmer's glue.

"Uh-oh," Jerry muttered. "I don't need a drink anymore. Not inside this place."

"We must have come through a side entrance."

Jerry spun an about-face.

"Wait a minute." Hal grabbed his friend's arm. "Remember, we're here on official business."

"Oh yeah." Jerry grinned. "Let's drop a poster on the librarian and find an *official* water fountain."

The bottom floor was split-level, making the main entrance and information desk up a half flight of stairs. A petite woman wearing a green sweater glanced up from a computer screen. Her name tag read Ms. Garza.

"I'll be with you gentlemen in a moment."

Gentleman? Hal suppressed a laugh as he viewed the long room.

In the center, towering racks of books and periodicals spread out in orderly rows. Along each wall, patrons sat quietly at online workstations and study tables. Others read alone, parked in cubicles or lounged in comfortable chairs beside huge, tinted windows.

Outside, Hal saw a cluster of students laughing and talking. They stood in the shade near the same spot where

Bratton accused him and Jerry of disturbing the peace. In the street, a giant blinking arrow diverted traffic around a road repair crew, while workers broke up chunks of asphalt with a jackhammer.

"Yes?" Ms. Garza peered over her reading glasses.

"May we hang a reward poster?" Hal held up the stack of posters. "We're working for Chief Nelson."

"Part-time," Jerry added. "Where's the water fountain?"

Ms. Garza raised her eyebrows. "I'll answer one question at a time. Young man, what does this announcement concern?"

Hal handed her one of the orange sheets.

"Hmm. This morning I overheard students talking about how their bicycles were stolen. What a terrible thing. Criminal."

"Yes, ma'am," Hal agreed, remembering his manners.

"Next, they'll be stealing our library books."

"Only the good ones," Jerry added.

Hal punched him with his elbow.

She glanced at her computer screen, then concentrated on the boys. "Do you have many notices to distribute?"

"Lots." Hal cleared his throat. "We need to hurry."

"Plus, find a water fountain," Jerry added.

Mrs. Garza eyed Jerry's shirt. "It appears you already have." She chuckled and checked the poster's backside. "Good. There's the proper stamp. Any printed material posted on this campus *must* be approved. You wouldn't believe what students try and get away with."

"We wouldn't?" Jerry wrinkled his nose.

"You would not." Ms. Garza removed her glasses. "You boys work part-time for Chief Nelson?"

"Yes, ma'am," Hal replied, more polite than before. He glanced wearily at Jerry. "My older brother, Rick Tanner, is editor of *The Cutlass*. Chief Nelson asked him to—"

"Rick threw the job at us." Jerry patted the desktop. "We're gonna stick little orange signs up all over town ... for free."

"I see." Ms. Garza smiled. "Tell your brother he's a fine journalist."

"Sure ... uh ... ma'am." Hal reached for the poster. "Where do you want it?"

She considered the question before pointing toward the front of the library. "Face out, attached to the inside glass on the middle door. The weather can't destroy the paper, and the tape is easy to remove. There's nothing harder than detaching adhesive exposed to harsh outdoor elements."

"That's good to know." Hal wished the librarian would hurry with her instructions.

"Also, anyone entering through the main entrance will notice." She handed Hal four pieces of scotch tape. Her smile returned.

Hal taped while Jerry steadied the poster. The glass felt warm against his fingers, while the frigid air-conditioning made him shiver. No wonder Ms. Garza wore a sweater.

Her sweater.

"Hey, Jerry? This building's air-conditioned."

"Duh, Dude. Aren't they all?"

Hal's heart raced. "Look at those students outside joking around," he whispered. "See the guy with the jackhammer."

"Okay."

"What do you hear?"

"Nothing."

"Yes," Hal shouted. "This building is soundproof."

"Shhh." Ms. Garza placed a finger over her lips and glared in their direction.

Hal continued in a hushed tone. "Remember when Bratton commanded us to stay away from here?"

"How could I forget?"

"He said we made too much noise. Students complained."

"Yeah?"

"Bratton scolded us 'cause no one could study."

"Don't remind me."

"Jerry?" Hal rolled his eyes. "There's no way we sounded louder than a jackhammer. We didn't bother anybody. The cop lied."

Furrows formed on Jerry's forehead. "Why would Bratton invent a reason to keep us away from ... a library?"

"Don't know, but I'll bet he fibbed about the vacant building too."

Hal finished taping, then stood back to check if the poster was straight. He read the bold stamp, *SSU Approved*, on the backside.

"Hey," he yelled. "Why didn't I notice sooner?"

Before Ms. Garza responded, Hal scooped up the stack of orange posters and shot out of the main entrance in a dead run.

"What about my drink?" Jerry tried his best to keep up.

Hal sped past the math building and another dorm. The vacant building stood less than a hundred yards away. *If my theory proves correct, Bratton is guilty of a second whopper.*

Reaching the shade of a leafy magnolia tree, Hal paused to catch his breath. Their skateboards remained in the distance, untouched. Bratton was nowhere in sight.

"What's ... the matter ... with you?" Jerry heaved, gasping for air. "Are you ... insane?" He collapsed on the ground in a sweaty heap.

"I need to look at the *Building Closed* sign. C'mon."

Jerry struggled to his feet and followed. They soon disappeared behind the cedar hedge where Wiley hid when he'd turned on the sprinklers. The spot lay no more than ten feet from the sign.

"This old building ... gives me ... the creeps," Jerry said between breaths.

"Stay outta sight and keep a look out for Bratton's car." Hal dumped the stack of posters and scuttled up the steps to the vacant building.

"Not fun. I'm wilting with thirst and you wanna play detective. I'll sue for friend abuse."

"Hey, Jer. The sign's made outta paper."

"I'm unimpressed."

"Attached on the outside of the door."

"Still thirsty."

"Hasn't faded."

"I am."

"Bratton swore the sign was here for months. The tape looks new."

As Hal expected, the tape released with ease. He flipped the sign over, studied the back, then replaced it in the same spot.

"Hurry up, Hal. Someone's coming."

Hal leaped down the steps and ducked behind the hedge. Deep in conversation. two students carrying backpacks ambled by.

"The sign's not official," Hal said when all was clear. "It's a fake."

"What do you mean?"

He flipped over a reward poster and massaged the approval stamp. "Remember what Rick and Ms. Garza said about this stamp? The back of the *Building Closed* sign is blank."

"Some hilarious joke," Jerry grumbled. "We were almost jailbirds 'cause of a dumb prank."

Hal shivered. "Bratton posted the sign, or at least knows who did."

Jerry barely spoke. "How do you know?"

"If the sign's legit, the cop wouldn't have cut us a speck of slack. He'd haul us to the police station and call our parents. Officer Bratton wants to keep us away from this old building."

"And the library."

"Exactly. He spied on us yesterday, then followed us here."

"Yeah. And Bratton … or somebody … put up the fake sign last night." Jerry was on a roll.

"A sign meant to scare us away if we came back today. When we didn't see it, the cop got nervous and dragged us to Rick."

THE GLITTER EFFECT

Jerry's eyes widened. "First the library. Now, this crummy place. Why?"

Hal sighed. "One way or another ... we're gonna find out."

CHAPTER FIVE: MAJOR CLUE

The Jolly Roger served the best pizza and cheeseburgers on the drag. Owner Roger Horton was the most renowned running back to play football at Southern State University.

"I'm glad your dad and Jolly Roger were teammates." Jerry snatched the last slice of pizza. "You're lucky."

"Why?" Hal hadn't eaten a bite of his piece. There was too much on his mind to bother with lunch. When he'd voiced a silent *thank you* to God for the food, which was his habit at school, he'd also asked for help dealing with Officer Bratton, and whatever else happened.

"Why? Duh, Dude. Your dad played football with a famous guy. The Pirates won back-to-back national titles." Jerry sprinkled on a gob of red pepper, then reached for the jar of grated Parmesan. He unscrewed the lid and dumped out half the contents.

Hal scrunched his face. Parmesan cheese smelled like baby burp.

"Isn't the nickname 'cause he laughed every time he scored a touchdown?" Jerry stuffed the entire piece into his mouth.

"Who? My Dad?"

"Nuh-wuh. Joweey-Woger-Worton," Jerry said between chews.

Hal knew he should have waited to go to the bathroom. While he was gone, Jerry ordered one of Jolly Roger's *Smash-mouth* pizzas. It consisted of classic tomato sauce with mozzarella cheese but was topped with bits of hot dog, popcorn, peanuts, French fries, jalapeños, sauerkraut, and dill pickles. The flavor combination mirrored snacks available at a football game.

Jerry swallowed, then belched. "If I owned this place, I'd serve a breakfast pizza covered with a hundred kinds of cereal."

Ignoring his friend's chatter, Hal took a long drink of cola. "What do a library and a vacant classroom building have in common?"

"Beats me." Jerry eyed Hal's plate. "Gonna eat your slice?"

"Other people hang around those two buildings. Why did Bratton pick on us?"

"Probably 'cause we're kids. He figures we'll do something dumb." Jerry took the empty pizza pan and slurped off the leftover sauce. A reddish blob of popcorn stuck to the end of his nose.

Hal laughed. Jerry looked like Rudolph. The image shoved his mind in a different direction—*Rudolph the Red-Nosed Reindeer. Misunderstood, yet in the end, a winner.* "Still a hero," Hal whispered.

"Speak up, dude." Jerry eyed Hal's plate. "What'd you say?"

"Bratton's jealous. He wants to solve the bicycle case and get the glory."

"Plus the reward money." Jerry licked his lips. "If you're not gonna eat your pizza, could I ...? Thanks."

Another idea sizzled. "When Bratton yelled at us outside the library and vacant building, we were the only ones there, right?"

"Except Wiley. Would you hand me the mustard? And the honey?"

Hal slid his friend the condiments. "Bratton must have a lead in the case. He's probably discovered evidence involving those two buildings and doesn't want us watching."

"Or Wiley looking at stuff either." Jerry slathered on a thick coating of each, and smothered the pizza with more red pepper and the rest of the Parmesan.

Hal drained his glass. The fact Bratton wouldn't want Wiley getting any ideas and becoming another hero made sense. But what—if anything—did an empty building and a library have to do with missing bicycles?

He peered across the table. Jerry wore a honey-mustard mustache.

"Come on." Hal tossed across a wad of napkins. "Wipe your face and we're outta here. Need to find what Bratton knows. Maybe while hanging reward posters, we'll discover a clue."

"Or several."

Hal called back to his friend. "Let's keep our eyes open."

Merchants along the Drag were eager to hang reward posters in their shops. The owner of Sands'n Subs complained how two of her employees had bicycles stolen the previous evening while making dorm deliveries.

A student working at Captain Cooks Coffee & Cappuccino said his bike disappeared during a night class.

The manager of Buccaneer Books wanted posters placed on both floors.

Back on campus, the boys worked throughout the afternoon. They rode their skateboards from building to building, distributed posters, asked questions. Everyone they met hoped the reward earned results, however, no one had witnessed anything unusual. Students who'd lost bikes offered scant information.

However, one clue remained constant—all thefts occurred after dark. Two guys playing Frisbee joked the bikes performed a disappearing act once the sun set.

Whaaah. Whaaah. Whaaah.

"Snack time. Let's ride over to the student center and get a candy bar."

"Okay." Hal wanted to buy something to drink and review the facts. At night, the majority of SSU was well lit. Hordes of people gathered outside, enjoying activities amidst cool summer temps. How did hundreds of bicycles vanish without a trace?

Twenty yards from the student center, Jerry fell. Not a bad fall—a skinned knee and elbow.

At first, Hal thought his friend had lost his balance. The sidewalk leading down to the entrance was steep, especially for Jerry.

"My new watch," Jerry whined. "It's probably busted."

Hal picked up Jerry's board. "You've lost a wheel off your board."

Jerry pushed a few buttons, shook the watch, and wiped it on his T-shirt. "The crystal's scratched."

"Listen. Focus on what's important." Hal handed Jerry his board. "If we don't find your wheel, we're gonna be stuck walking."

Jerry groaned and pointed. "Something rolled through there."

Beside the spot where Jerry fell was a large grate.

Hal squatted and touched the rusty bars. "It's a storm drain. Looks deep."

"See if you can lift the grate."

"Can't." Hal grunted. "But I see the bottom—one of those concrete culverts big enough to walk through."

"What about my wheel?"

"I see leaves, broken glass, and a couple of faded gum wrappers. Wait. There's something round."

"My wheel?"

Kneeling, Hal leaned close, wedging his hands like binoculars between his eyes and the thick metal. "I see places where the concrete has disintegrated into dirt."

"The round thing? How big is it?"

"Oh wow. I don't believe it." Hal's cry echoed underground.

"What? Is my wheel busted?"

Hal straightened. His head swam, making it difficult for his eyes to focus. He'd asked for divine direction and received a significant clue. Perhaps God wanted them to help solve the case.

"What do you see?" Jerry rubbed his elbow.

"The dirt spots?"

"Yeah."

"They're covered with bicycle tracks."

CHAPTER SIX: SIXTEEN PACES

"Bicycle tracks?" Down there?" In two seconds flat, Jerry peered into the dimness.

"Genius." Hal wiped rust off his hand. "Whoever's stealing bikes is moving them through the underground drainage tunnels."

"To where?"

"How should I know? Probably a designated pick-up point." Hal folded his arms. "The system has to empty somewhere, maybe into a creek off-campus. No wonder the bikes disappear."

"How do they get 'em down there?"

Hal studied the grate. One side hinged like a door. The opposite edge had a latch welded shut. "No thief got in through here. Even without the grate, the opening's too small for a bike to fit."

Jerry blew a long sigh before flopping backward onto the grass. "I'll never get my wheel. If my parents have to buy me another skateboard, they'll gripe about the money until—"

"The money." Hal leaped to his feet as a sharp tingle vibrated the length of his spine. He felt the same sensation before riding a triple loop roller coaster. "I remember something, Jerry."

"How to find my wheel?"

"No. The reward money. A thousand bucks."

"So?"

"So forget about your stupid wheel. With that much cash, we get new boards, the best made. Take lessons. Buy the latest smartphones."

A grin widened Jerry's face. "Oh yeah, 'cause we know where the crooks are. All we have to do is tell the cops."

"Not yet," Hal countered. "Only when we're sure." An unexpected thought sprouted. A concept planted by his dad and watered by the truth—*Am I serving God or myself?*

"I'm not sure," Hal answered aloud.

"You're repeating yourself. I understand. We don't tell the cops until we're *sure* who made the bike tracks." Jerry grinned again. "So what's our plan?"

"Um ..." Hal pushed the *serving* thought aside and regained his composure. "We need to get into the drainage system and follow those tracks. There's bound to be another grate somewhere. One not welded shut."

"What if Bratton catches us?"

"No way. If he knew about the crooks moving bikes through the tunnels, he would've already arrested them."

"I sure hope he doesn't see us snooping around drainage grates. He might get suspicious."

Hal frowned. He'd not considered the possibility. Bratton may be spying on them now. "We've got to ask someone how to get down into the system. We'll say we're searching for your lost wheel—which is the truth."

Jerry rolled onto his stomach. He resembled a beached seal, a sweaty one. "Should work. Who'd know about storm drains and stuff?"

"Let's ask Wiley." Hal offered his hand to help Jerry up.

"Wiley?"

"Why not. He is a groundskeeper. I bet he knows every inch of this campus."

"How will we recognize him?"

"Easy. How many guys tramp around here in work pants and combat boots?"

The boys ditched their skateboards in an empty planter box near the student center.

They'd not walked far when Hal noticed towering sprays of water above a freshly mowed lawn. The flow stopped, then gushed again. "Look, Jer, Pirate Stadium. Bet Wiley's adjusting sprinklers."

"Where Jolly Roger Horton played football?"

"Yep. Along with my dad and a bunch of other old guys."

Jerry slowed to a stop. "Wow. Look how high the seats go. I'll bet this place holds a million people."

Hal kept moving. "Gawk later. We need to find Wiley."

"Maybe he's inside watering the playing field." Jerry trotted to catch up. "Let's go see. We can climb to the top of the upper deck."

Before Hal protested, a wiry man stepped out from behind a clump of pine trees. He wore a starched green maintenance uniform with sleeves rolled neatly above his elbows. A blue SSU baseball cap pushed back to reveal a military cut of white-blond hair. In one hand he carried a plastic sprinkler head. In the other, a large, muddy wrench. His boots gleamed in the afternoon sun.

Hal stopped. "Are you Wiley?"

The man smiled and nodded.

"I'm Hal Tanner, Rick's Tanner's brother. And this is my friend, Jerry Morris."

Jerry stuck out his hand. Wiley placed the mud-covered wrench in Jerry's palm, shook it, and cackled.

The boys exchanged glances. Jerry retrieved his hand.

Hal cleared his throat. "Um ... we wondered if you'd help us find something."

"Yeah. My lost skateboard wheel." Jerry wiped the mud on his T-shirt.

Wiley smiled again.

"Over by the student center is a steep hill where Jerry's board lost a wheel. We're pretty sure it rolled through a drainage grate. Thought you'd know how to get down into the underground system. Then we ..."

Wiley's friendly smile melted into a blank expression. His eyes wore a distant look. He didn't say a word.

"Then we'd find it," Hal finished. He remembered what Rick said about Wiley's head injury causing a condition called conduction aphasia. It affected speech. Maybe he couldn't answer.

"No problem, Wiley." Hal felt sorry for the guy. "We'll buy another wheel. Hope we didn't bother you."

"Chat-noo-ga," Wiley said slowly.

"Excuse me?"

"With Ch-Ch-Chat-nooga. Look out."

"Chattanooga?" Hal clarified.

"Uhm-yes."

"What's he saying?" Jerry whispered.

Wiley spoke faster. "J-Jollys R-Rogers loves. Jollys Rogers loves, umm-yes, s-sixteen paces souths."

Hal didn't know how to respond. What was Wiley trying to tell them?

Wiley aimed the wrench in the direction of the vacant building. "With big X. Marks sp-spot. Look out. See like a bird." His face flushed. "X marks spot."

"What spot?" Hal saw Wiley's frustration.

"With Ch-Chat-nooga," Wiley said louder. "Sixteens paces souths. L-L-Like a bird. Look out." Wiley aimed the wrench a second time, motioning with his head. "Ch-Chat-nooga. At Chat-nooga."

Both boys spun around to look. When they turned back, Wiley had disappeared.

Jerry scratched his head. "Where'd he go?"

"Isn't Chattanooga a city in Tennessee?"

"How should I know?"

"Wiley kept pointing in the direction of the vacant building and saying *Chattanooga*. Does he want us to go there?"

"Forget the whole idea, Hal. I'm not going to Tennessee. My mom will ground me till Christmas."

"What did Wiley mean by *X marks the spot* and *sixteen paces south*?"

"Dude watches too many pirate movies." Jerry sniffed the mud on his T-shirt. "Nothing better than the sweet aroma of football dirt. Let's go check out the field."

Hal stroked his chin. "He said *Jolly Roger loves*. Loves what?"

"Smash-mouth pizzas."

"Will you be serious?"

Jerry moved forward. "Nope. Serious ain't fun."

The stadium was unlocked, encouraging students to walk or jog around the track. A crumpled-up paper cup made a perfect miniature football. As Hal ran out for passes, he considered what Wiley said. His words had meaning, though sounded disconnected. Was he trying to tell them how to get down into the drainage system?

He kept saying *look out*.

Look out for what?

For whom?

Were he and Jerry in danger?

"Enough football for me." Jerry dried his face on a shirtsleeve. "Let's find a water fountain, before we climb to the nosebleed seats."

After a healthy drink, the boys followed the winding ramp to the top. With each step, Hal reviewed what Wiley said, or tried to say. Was his brain sending the wrong signals to his mouth? How frustrating to know something important, yet be unable to communicate the message.

How embarrassing.

As they ascended, the calm, afternoon air puffed into a steady breeze. Jerry rattled non-stop about football, while Hal's thoughts commanded a whirlwind mix of Bratton, mysterious buildings, drainage grates, bicycle tracks ... and Wiley. Hal hurt for the guy, yet there was no way to help make his life easier.

Unless ....

Another idea popped into Hal's brain. *If Jerry and I locate the crooks, then the pressure's off Bratton, and he'd treat Wiley better. I'd also be serving God.*

And, the reward money?

The one thousand dollar amount made Hal dizzy, which wasn't a good thing at the top of a football stadium. He placed the thought aside until later.

"Feels good up here." Hal panned his hand from left to right. "I can see across the entire campus."

"I'll bet we're twenty stories high." Jerry peered over the edge. "Let's have a spit race. Whoever hits the ground first, wins."

With a dry mouth, Hal didn't produce much.

However, Jerry hacked up a big glob. He could dredge up loogies on command. The guy was an excellent spitter.

Two things happened at once—the breeze stiffened, slinging the spitballs sideways, which caused Hal to see the X.

"There it is." Hal stepped to the rail for a better look. "I see the X."

Jerry had already gathered another mouthful. When he released it, a wind gust slung the wad back onto his face.

Hal pointed toward the vacant building. "It's those two sidewalks. See? They cross to form a big X. Wiley said to *look like a bird.* Up here we have a bird's eye view."

"You sure?" Jerry wiped his face on both sleeves. "What if there's a similar X?"

Hal remembered what he'd seen earlier in the week. "Come on. We're about to catch the crooks."

He bolted down the ramp. The giant X was located halfway between Pirate Stadium and the vacant building. By the time Jerry caught up, Hal was on his hands and knees at the spot where the sidewalks intersected.

"I'm getting ... tired of ... this. What are ... you doing?"

"It's right here. In the center of the X. Look."

Written in the cement were the words *Jolly Roger loves*.

Hal sat back on his haunches. "Whomever Jolly Roger loved was covered with new cement."

"What now?"

"Didn't Wiley say sixteen paces south?"

At twelve paces, the boys found an overgrown azalea bush. After closer inspection, it proved to be ten bushes planted in a tight circle. They crawled into the center of the azalea bed, completely hidden from view.

Jerry shrugged. "Maybe Wiley got his directions wrong."

"Not by a long shot. Sixteen paces would be underneath us." Hal found a stout stick and pushed it into the soft dirt. The stick sunk about six inches, then hit something hard.

Something hollow.

"Let's dig." The loose dirt allowed the boys to burrow with their hands. In minutes, they unearthed a rusted manhole cover measuring three feet in diameter.

Lookout Mountain Iron Works - Chattanooga, Tennessee was stamped in bold letters.

"Yes," Hal shouted.

Jerry's voice trembled slightly. "See if you can lift it."

With the stick, Hal managed to pry up an edge. "Quick. Find something else and jam it underneath."

The aid of another stick enabled both boys to squeeze their fingers beneath the lip of the cover.

"Good," Hal panted. "On the count of three, pull with everything you've got."

"One."

"Two."

"Three."

The heavy cover flipped onto the dirt. The middle of the azalea bed was now an opening to a deep, dark, gaping hole.

Hal crawled to the edge and poked his head below ground level. The cool air smelled stale. A ladder led down into the blackness below. "No one's used this entrance for years. Look at all those beautiful cobwebs."

"Are you crazy?" Jerry rocked back on the mound of soft earth. "Ain't nothing pretty about spiders."

"We'll call this place *Chattanooga*." Hal patted the cover. "It's our secret way into the system."

"We still don't know how the crooks get the bikes down there."

Hal felt the familiar tingle. "Doesn't matter. Our plan is to follow the tracks. We'll sneak back here tonight after Rick goes to sleep."

"With a big, flaming torch. It'll scare off the spiders." Jerry shivered.

"Under Rick's bed."

"Spiders?"

"A powerful flashlight."

"A torch is better." Jerry frowned. "How about food?"

"We won't be gone long."

"What if we can't find my wheel?"

"Don't worry. By this time tomorrow, the reward money will be ours."

CHAPTER SEVEN: CONCRETE TUNNELS

Rick had to work after hours, so slipping away from him unnoticed wasn't an issue.

After the boys ate a late evening snack, they exited the apartment. Fifteen minutes later, they descended into the chasm called Chattanooga.

"Ouch," Hal's whisper was louder than he intended. "There's no room on this skinny ladder for my hand and your foot."

Jerry inched up a step. "Why are we whispering?"

"The bike thieves, remember? Sound echoes easily down here. We don't want them to hear us."

"Good point. When do I get to hold the flashlight?"

"Later." Hal reached the bottom, positioning the light where they could see. "Wow. This place is a cave."

"I hope there are no bats." Jerry stepped off the last rung and looked around. "Spiders are bad enough."

They stood in a narrow underground room, surrounded on three sides by high rock walls. Much of the mortar had crumbled, leaving tiny dunes along the edge of a rough stone floor. Where the rocks ended, a concrete tunnel loomed into the blackness ahead.

Hal gulped. "Matches the culvert where you lost your wheel. I bet we're in a side tunnel leading into the main system."

Jerry blew an airy whistle. "Sure is creepy down here. Maybe we ought to come back when we have two flashlights."

"We're fine." Something eerie gently rapped on the rear window of Hal's innermost thoughts—mostly a feeling. Perhaps the tap wasn't gentle.

They inched along the culvert making as little noise as possible. At first, the bottom appeared level, before the floor sloped downward. Scattered throughout were bits of paper, plastic trash, dead leaves, and pine needles. In areas where the concrete crumbled and left dirt, they saw no tracks.

"It's because we're in a side tunnel." Hal shined his light in a wide arc. "I'll bet when we reach the main artery there are plenty of tracks."

The culvert soon emptied into a second rock-walled room. Three new tunnels fanned out in different directions.

"Which way now?" Jerry stepped beside Hal.

Hal directed light into the openings of each new passage. "That one's biggest and looks the flattest. The other two slant upward. Bet they're the offshoots."

"So?"

"So ... the big one must be part of the main system. It's where we'll find bike tracks."

"And my wheel."

The larger tunnel was anything but flat, and not as straight as the one from Chattanooga. The path dipped and rose without warning, snaked into a series of sharp turns, before connecting with other passageways.

"Great," Hal murmured when they reached the third fork. "I'd better mark our trail. We don't wanna get lost on the way back." With a pebble, he scratched a small arrow at the base of the culvert. "There. A secret reminder. Wish I'd marked the first two."

They continued at the pace of curious snails, carefully inspecting each patch of dirt. The farther they traveled the cooler the air, fringed with moisture. Huge cobwebs draped across fittings where one culvert connected to the next. Hal felt swallowed by an evil, earthen monster.

"Did I mention I don't get along with spiders?" Jerry spoke in half voice. "Especially big ones."

Hal squatted, studying an area where the dirt collected. "Nothing." He wagged his head. "Makes me wonder if we imagined those bike tracks this afternoon. Why haven't we passed under any drainage grates?"

Jerry pushed a button, making his watch glow. "Ten thirty-six. We've been down here for over thirty minutes. My turn to carry the light."

"Okay." Hal took a deep breath. "Let's backtrack to the second rock room and check out a different tunnel. Be sure to follow the arrows."

With Jerry in the lead, they trudged in reverse. The thought of failure made Hal cringe. If they traveled the other tunnels and came up empty, it meant zero rewards, which equaled wasted valuable time.

Time spent practicing his skateboarding.

Time becoming *best* at something.

Anything.

Rick never wasted a minute. He was a winner.

Jerry's sudden shout burst into Hal's thoughts. "Hal. Look."

High overhead was a metal grate, identical to where Jerry lost his wheel.

Hal dropped his gaze to the culvert floor. He spoke in hushed tones. "There's the same broken glass I saw earlier ... and gum wrappers." He faced his friend. "I don't know how, but you've led us into the main system.

Jerry gave him a thumbs-up. "Bet my wheel's here too."

"So are the bike tracks. Hand me the flashlight."

"Not until I find my wheel."

"Jerry?"

"No."

"Forget about your stupid wheel." Hal spit the words through clenched teeth. He grabbed the front end of the flashlight. "We'll buy the best boards made and take lessons. Remember?"

"It's still my turn. Let go."

"You let go."

Jerry kept his grip. "Don't want lessons. I need to find—"

"Shh. Lower your voice."

"You're the one shoutin'."

Before Hal spoke again, the flashlight lay dark on the hard concrete floor, smashed beyond repair. He was the one who'd tried to snatch the light. Why was Jerry so stubborn about an inexpensive skateboard wheel?

A long silence followed, as frightening as the smothering blackness. Hal couldn't see Jerry's face, though heard sniffles.

"I'm sorry." Hot tears of hopelessness filled Hal's eyes. Why would this happen when he tried to serve God?

Jerry's voice trembled. "What are we gonna do?"

There was no easy solution. Without light, they'd never get back to Chattanooga. They could stand under the grate and scream for help until someone heard, but the noise would scare off the crooks.

Unless ...

The crooks found them first.

A massive wave of nausea crested and crashed inside Hal's stomach. He hadn't considered the possibility. He didn't want to imagine ...

"Help us, God," Hal uttered. "Please help us."

More silence.

A faint echo. A hollow clicking noise.

"What's that sound?" Jerry whispered.

"Shh."

The clicking became more distinct.

Louder.

Closer.

Hal's knees grew weak. "It's bicycle gears. Don't move."

The clicks soon mingled with an echo of muffled voices—deep tones sprinkled with what sounded like ... glee.

The echoes soon waned, floating in another direction. Hal blew a short sigh of relief—until he saw a speck of light.

Deep into the blackness flashed a tiny circle of white. The light was much too weak to shine far, nor strong enough to illuminate the floor, nor cast a shadow. Yet ample to navigate a stolen bicycle through the maze of underground passages.

Hal hoped the crooks hadn't heard them. Plus, he and Jerry needed to hide.

Fast.

How could they see?

If the flashlight worked, the beam would reveal their whereabouts.

The sounds and light grew stronger, no more than fifty yards away. In less than a minute the bright dot would reach out and part the curtain of protective darkness. Now was the time to act.

Hal breathed directions into Jerry's ear. "Grab the back of my shirt. Don't make a sound."

Jerry hung on as Hal groped his way along the gritty wall. Minutes before the flashlight fiasco, they'd avoided tripping over big chunks of cement where a portion of the culvert's side collapsed. Hal couldn't remember if enough rubble remained to hide behind.

Enough was their only hope.

The boys moved in slow motion. Hal reached hand over hand, trying not to bump his head on a jagged piece of concrete. Places where mud collected and dried broke loose, tumbling into his eyes and down the collar of his T-shirt. Sticky cobwebs stuck to his hair and slung across his face.

The voices grew louder. The leading edge of light crept closer.

Come on, where's the debris?

Hal tried to work faster. Pulling Jerry along was like towing a lead statue.

The light paused. Words about "a break" mumbled into broken sentences. Laughter erupted.

Good. If they stop to rest, it will buy us time.

Hal banged his right shin, hard. Pain exploded up his leg and splintered throughout his body. He bit his tongue and gagged, fighting back the urge to vomit. Except he'd stumbled into what was most needed—a slight depression behind a concrete pile where dirt washed away during past thunderstorms. Hal dove into the shallow hole and pulled Jerry down. Light instantly lit the area above them. They were safe in the shadow of the rubble.

Several feet from Hal's face a bicycle rolled past—then another. He couldn't tell much about the two men who walked the bikes, except something one of them said must've been hilarious. In seconds the light vanished. Their jollity faded into silence.

The boys waited in frozen nothingness. Hal couldn't see his hand in front of his face. For all he knew, Jerry fainted from fear. Neither boy spoke, nor moved.

Hal felt the hair rise on the back of his neck.

He'd heard nothing.

The darkness—changed.

An element added.

Another presence.

Hal wanted to scream, but his mouth refused to work. When he tried to move, fear bound him in an invisible straitjacket.

Something cold and dull poked him in the back.

A voice whispered, "Gotcha."

CHAPTER EIGHT: STRANGE GARBAGE

The whisper erupted into Wiley's broad laugh. "G-Gotcha," he repeated. Gotcha. Lost wheel." He poked the hard plastic into Hal's neck and shook with amusement.

Hal still couldn't speak. Half of his heart stuck in his throat. The other half leaped up inside his head and beat his brain.

"F-found one lost wheel, two lost boys." Wiley put his hand on Hal's shoulder. "Hold my belt. Come with m-me."

Hal felt hurled in slow motion through an endless black fog. Minutes passed before he realized Jerry still clutched the back of his shirt. Wiley led them quickly through the pitch-dark tunnels. By the time Hal's head cleared, he and Jerry climbed up the ladder at Chattanooga. The skateboard wheel lay beside the manhole cover.

Wiley had disappeared.

The boys crawled outside the ring of azalea bushes into the soft, moonlit night. Exhausted, they sprawled on the plush lawn. Millions of stars blinked overhead. The air never smelled sweeter. In the distance stood the ominous silhouette of the vacant building.

Jerry sighed and checked his watch. "It's twenty minutes till midnight." He examined the tough plastic wheel, thumped it, making it spin. "I thought we were goners. Good thing you said a prayer."

"You heard?" Hal assumed he'd prayed silently.

"I'm not deaf. Glad God isn't too busy to listen."

"Me, too."

Jerry's family didn't attend church, so Hal invited his friend to several youth lock-ins, which included a Bible study. Jerry enjoyed the games and loved the food, but never mentioned a word about anything else.

"We were doomed till Wiley found us." Jerry lolled his head back and forth on the grass. "Trapped in total darkness. Reminds me of the guy who got swallowed by a whale."

"Jonah?"

"Yeah. There's no light inside a fish's belly. Stinks too." Jerry scrunched his nose. "S'pose God had Wiley rescue us?"

"Positive."

"Same as when the whale spits up Jonah."

"Right."

Jerry hooted. "Makes the dude a giant loogie."

The boys chuckled at the image, which improved their mood.

"Wiley must have seen the cover off Chattanooga and figured we were lost."

"How'd he find us without a light?"

"I don't know," Hal said, which led him to an immediate thought—an uncomfortable notion souring his mood. He was ashamed to consider the idea, especially after what they'd discussed. "Listen, if we see Wiley, don't say anything about the bicycle thieves."

"How come? Will he tell Bratton?"

"No way. Though it bothers me how well he knew his way around down there. I wonder if he's in on—" Hal bit his lip.

Wiley stepped out of the shadows holding two plastic bottles of cola ... ice-cold.

"Thanks." Jerry unscrewed the top. "And for finding my wheel."

Hal forced a smile. "Also rescuing us." He hoped his suspicions of Wiley as a crook weren't overheard.

Wiley nodded, opened his mouth to speak, then sat. He stuttered something, paused, spoke again. "T-tunnels getting too old and dangerous. N-not the same when I was a boy."

Hal sat up straight. An idea flickered in his pile of clues. "Since your dad was a professor, you grew up on this campus, right?"

"Uhm-yes."

"So I'll bet you played in the drainage system a lot, I mean as a kid. You probably have each tunnel memorized."

Wiley punctuated his grin with a single clap.

Jerry cocked his head. "Explains why you didn't need a flashlight."

"Is the drainage grate over by the student center welded shut to keep people out?" Hal swished a mouthful of cola, making it fizz around his bottom teeth. Wiley's childhood at SSU made sense, explaining his knowledge of the underground passages. Perhaps he was searching for Jerry's wheel, *and* the two of them.

"They're all w-welded shut. Several years back. All f-five grates."

Jerry motioned toward Chattanooga. "That one's not closed?"

"*Somebody* r-raked dirt over the cover. Made a flower bed." Wiley puffed out his chest.

The boys chuckled.

Wiley relaxed—his speech close to normal.

"Why a manhole cover instead of a grate?" Hal took another drink of his cola.

"An entrance for workers. System was built b-back during the Great Depression."

Hal remembered studying the dark period in America's past, a time spanning the 1930s when thousands of people lost their jobs, and there was little money. "I wrote a report about the Great Depression. My great-grandfather left home at sixteen, lied about his age, and worked for the WPA. I can't remember what the initials mean."

"Wants Pie Anytime?" Jerry rubbed his stomach.

Everyone laughed.

"Works Projects Administration." Wiley leaned toward Jerry. Provided c-construction jobs.

Jerry drained his can. "Why are the tunnels so big?" He ended his question with a loud burp.

Wiley cackled. "B-big 'cause this is a coastal area. Floods often, 'cept in a drought."

Hal and Jerry nodded in agreement.

In the distance, a garbage truck rattled past. Its red and amber taillights disappeared behind the vacant building.

"Not good." Wiley clinched his fists. "N-not good."

The clang of a metal dumpster echoed through the night. Wiley jerked an ear toward the sound, jumped to his feet, and stared across the lawn. His body rigid, as if standing at attention. "G-garbage whens there's no garbage," his tone strained. "Garbage when there's n-no garbages."

Unsure what to say, Hal stood too. Was this another one of Wiley's practical jokes?

Wiley inched backward. "Garbages whens there's no garbages. Stays away ... aways."

"Away from what?" Jerry shrugged one shoulder.

Pointing toward the vacant building, Wiley frowned. "There. Ands the t-tunnels. Should of n-evers told. Too dangerous. I'm s-sorrys. I'm sorry." He slipped into the shadows.

Hal snapped his fingers into a fist. "I knew it. Something odd is going on with the vacant building. Did you see how he stared?"

"Yeah, and did you catch the warning?" Jerry stood and faced Hal. "He said *stay away*. Keep out of the tunnels too, which is fine with me 'cause I hate spiders and the smell of fish belly. Let's go back to Rick's apartment and get something to eat."

A metal bang echoed from another dumpster. "What'd he mean about *garbage when there's no garbage*?" Hal studied the vacant building.

"Who cares? Listen, we've already checked that spooky place and it's bad luck. There's nothing but a bunch of empty rooms nobody uses."

Hal slapped his best friend on the back. "You're brilliant. Come on."

The boys scampered across the starlit lawn. Except for a narrow service road and loading platform, the area behind the vacant building supported dense woods. Squeezed onto the platform sat four large, steel dumpsters. Hal and Jerry watched from the shadows as the garbage truck released the fourth dumpster and roared away.

"Sure is a large amount of trash from a building no one uses."

Jerry glowed. "My theory?"

"Mostly."

"Hey, I am intelligent."

"Okay, Einstein. Tell me where all this garbage is from?"

Jerry climbed onto the loading platform and flipped back one of the duel lids on the first dumpster. "Whatever was in here doesn't stink."

Joining him, Hal stood on tip-toes and took a deep whiff. "Smells of cardboard boxes. I think I see a roll of duct tape."

The boys raised the other lid to allow more moonlight. "Duct tape all right." Jerry held up the lid. "Pieces are stuck to the floor." He lowered the lid without slamming it.

Hal checked inside the other three bins. "They smell of cardboard too. This first one has the most tape. Give me a boost. I'll climb inside."

Lacing both hands under Hal's foot, Jerry shoved him over the edge.

"The strips of tape have thin layers of cardboard stuck to them."

"See anything else?"

"A few cigarette butts." Hal looked closer. "Hey, wait a minute. Oh shoot, it's burned out."

"What?"

"It's a penlight." He produced what resembled a fat ink pen. "See the tiny bulb on the end?"

Jerry yawned. "Too bad we didn't have one down in the tunnels."

"The bike crooks did."

Headlights swooped around the side of the vacant building. A radio blared country music.

"Quick." Hal ducked down. "Climb in."

Jerry tried to hoist himself over the edge, but his stomach caught.

"Give me your hands."

Hal yanked as Jerry jumped. On the second try, they tumbled onto the metal floor with a thud.

The headlights beamed a final turn as tires screeched to a stop beside the loading platform. Music played another minute, then died with the engine. A car door opened and slammed.

The boys slowly raised their eyes above the metal edge. "Oh no," Jerry muttered. "It's Bratton. What's he doing here?"

"I bet he's searching for clues. Those he doesn't want anyone else to discover."

Jerry's voice trembled. "I sure hope he doesn't find us."

Bratton reached through the open driver's side window, grabbed a flashlight, and tromped toward the platform.

THE GLITTER EFFECT

Icy sweat peppered Hal's forehead. If Bratton peered into dumpsters, catching the boys would be easier than finding gum stuck under a table in the school cafeteria.

Instead, the cop focused on the ground, examining every square inch of pavement, babbling something under his breath.

Hal couldn't distinguish the words.

Finally, Bratton clicked off his light and climbed onto the platform. Both boys hit the deck. The cop continued to babble, stopping near the open dumpster where Hal and Jerry hid.

"So, they see me as a fool," Bratton seethed. "Think they're gonna get away clean." He snorted.

"I've got news for those buffoons. Know exactly what they're about. No one messes with a professional."

Bratton thumped his slimy cigar butt into the dumpster, and slammed both lids.

CHAPTER NINE: THE LETTER

The next morning, Hal awoke to crunching sounds and the theme music to an old *Indiana Jones* movie.

"Want some?" Jerry presented a jumbo box of sugarcoated cereal. "Is there any more chocolate milk?"

Hal squinted. "What time is it?"

Jerry checked his wrist. "A couple of minutes past ten. I'm glad Rick gets this classic movie channel. You wanna watch Harrison Ford escape from danger?"

Hal groaned. The last thing he wanted to see was a guy running for his life. With Indiana Jones, the situation often included fighting off snakes. Bats and spiders, no problem. But snakes ...

Pushing with his elbows, Hal ooched into a half-sitting position against the back of the hide-a-bed. Before falling asleep he'd wrestled with the idea of telling Rick everything. In the night, fragments of the previous day's events twisted together into a horrific dream.

The boys skateboarded through the underground tunnels at a high rate of speed. Jerry's watch sounded, the alarm mimicking an earsplitting dinner bell instead of a baby's cry. He sped to Chattanooga for something to eat. Hal followed but was unable to keep up. Around the next bend, he realized he was lost. A posted sign read: *Chattanooga, Sixteen Paces South.* When he stopped to see if it bore the proper stamp, Bratton's patrol car appeared. The faster Hal skated, the faster the cop drove. Hal would've escaped, but the tunnel ended, trapping him in front of a rock wall. Instead of Bratton, Ms. Garza stepped out of the patrol car. She immediately morphed into Rick. He clutched a giant trophy for rescuing his little brother from another screw-up.

Hal pushed away the nightmare. "How long have you been awake?"

"An hour." Jerry fingered another handful of cereal. "Rick called. Said he couldn't meet us for lunch."

"Why?"

"Didn't explain. He wants Sleeping Beauty to call back," Jerry mocked. "Good thing there's a landline." He stuffed his mouth.

Hal scooted out of the hide-a-bed and stumbled across the living room into the adjoining kitchen. "Where's the phone?"

"In the fridge. Rang right in the middle of my run for peanut butter and bologna. I only have two hands."

Hal frowned. *Yeah, and three stomachs.* Opening the door, he grabbed the cold phone and punched his brother's number. "May I speak to Rick Tanner please ... oh, it's you."

"Hey, little brother." Rick only called him *little brother* when he was happy.

"Are you still at the newspaper?" Hal tried to sound awake.

"Sorry I never made it home last night. I ended crashing on an old couch in the press room."

"Aren't you tired?"

"Should be. I'm on an adrenalin high. Got a major scoop on the bike case this morning."

Hal's groggy brain jerked into reality. "What is it?"

"The info came from an anonymous caller."

"Male or female?"

"Who are you, Sherlock Holmes?" Rick chuckled. "The voice sounded disguised. Besides, I can't reveal a source. Ever heard of reporter ethics?"

"I guess so."

"Good. I'm gonna have to cancel lunch today. Gotta wait by the office phone for another tip. The caller will only talk to me and refuses to call my cell."

"Cool." Hal used his best vanilla tone, once more feeling the disappointment of their parents not allowing *him* to have a cell phone.

"This deal is enormous. I smell another journalism award."

Hal rubbed his icy palm across his pajama pants. "Listen. Stuff happened yesterday you'd wanna know—"

"What? You guys run into Bratton? I told you to stay away from him."

"Didn't see us."

"Good. Oops, got an incoming call. Perhaps it's the big one. Whatever you did this time will have to wait. Go out to the box and bring in yesterday's mail. Bye."

Hal's stomach hurt. Rick should thank them for hanging the reward posters. What they *did* was solve the crime of the summer ... almost. On track with everything else Hal tried in his life, *almost* never won a real trophy.

He dressed, retrieved the mail, sat crossed-legged on the living room floor, and thumbed through it. The stack contained junk ads, a few bills, and a letter addressed to him in his mom's handwriting.

Embarrassing. No one mailed old-fashioned stationery to kids.

If I had a cool cell phone, she could text.

Hal tore open the envelope. Inside was news concerning happenings at home. The letter ended with a P.S. reminding

Hal to change his underwear daily and mind his older brother. In addition was a page torn from a coloring book—a unicorn Bethany decorated with an enormous amount of glitter. Much of it wasn't glued and floated onto the carpet.

Great. Now I'll have to vacuum.

"Did we finish the salsa and tortilla chips?" Jerry was in the midst of another trek for treats during a commercial. "Tastes awesome with chocolate ice cream."

"On top of the fridge." Hal held up Bethany's page. "Careful. You walked through a pile of glitter. It gets everywhere."

"I don't see anything."

"'Cause, the light in here's not bright enough." Hal leaned forward and swung open the front door. Sunlight streamed inside. "See. There's glitter stuck to the bottom of your feet. And now you've tracked a million specks all the way into the kitchen."

"Sorry, Mr. Clean. I didn't know." Jerry went to the table. "Hey? Who ate all the chips and salsa?"

Hal closed the door. The disappointment he felt wasn't Jerry's fault. "Listen, at home, Bethany uses gobs of glitter, then tracks it all over the house. When enough light hits, bam. You're blinded from the sparkle. Mom calls it *The Glitter Effect.*"

"*The Glitter Effect.* My shiny route to the food." Jerry opened the freezer. "Who ate all the ice cream?"

"Jer." Hal dropped the unicorn and leaped to his feet. "The Glitter Effect isn't your route to the food."

"No?"

"It's our path to the bike crooks. Our *secret* trail."

Jerry spun an about-face. "Explain."

"First, we buy Rick another powerful flashlight."

"I'm only paying for half."

"Fine." Hal continued. "Next, we locate a craft store and get packages of silver glitter—it reflects best."

"Then what?"

"We dump a handful through each of the five drainage grates. You follow?"

"I don't want to." Jerry slammed the freezer shut and trudged empty-handed back to the hide-a-bed.

"After dark, we give the crooks long enough to walk a few bikes through the system and create a reflective trail."

"What if they notice the glitter?"

"A pen light's not strong enough to reach the culvert floor."

"Oh, yeah." Jerry plopped down on the bed. "Our new flashlight—"

"Plenty bright," Hal finished. "Once we're back underground, we'll begin at the second rock room."

"Where we first messed up."

"This time's different." Hal sat next to his friend. "Choosing the correct tunnel will be a cinch with all the little shiny dots. All we do is follow the glitter until we find where the bikes are hauled out of the system. Simple."

Jerry frowned. "Wiley warned us not to go back down there."

"Do you want a smartphone?"

"What if we meet the crooks?"

Hal rubbed his chin. "We'd been down in the tunnels for forty-five minutes when you asked to carry the flashlight."

"Right."

"We hid ten minutes later."

"Okay."

"Which means the crooks passed under the grate by the student center around eleven PM."

"I guess."

"After we climbed out of Chattanooga, you checked your watch—midnight."

"Twenty till," Jerry corrected.

"Which gives us a safe window of operation between eleven-fifteen and midnight."

"A window?"

"A time to go back underground. The crooks will have passed through the system and are back out stealing more bikes."

Jerry's face tightened, then relaxed. "All right, dude. I'm in."

"Good. We'll return to Chattanooga tonight—eleven o'clock sharp. Let's grab our boards and get to work."

"Only 'cause there's no more snacks."

Hal knew his explanation sounded logical, recalling several students who'd suffered stolen bikes the hour before midnight. But what if the crooks decided to follow a different schedule?

And what if there were more than two?

Then solving the case escalated into a dangerous challenge.

The final test to be the best ...

An exam Hal Tanner was desperate to pass.

CHAPTER TEN: SECRET PLAN

In less than an hour, the boys purchased their supplies and peered through the grate where Jerry lost his wheel.

Hal studied the culvert floor. "I see the same gum wrappers."

"Sure hope Bratton's not watching." Jerry raised his head and scanned the general area. "Maybe we should've left our boards back at the apartment."

"Relax. The cop's nowhere in sight. Hand me the glitter before somebody comes."

A powerful new flashlight and several small containers of silver glitter were hidden inside one of Rick's old backpacks.

Hal opened a packet and dumped half the contents through the grate. "I hope it's enough to make a trail. If we use too much, the crooks might notice."

Jerry pressed his face against the sun-warmed steel. "I can't tell you poured any down there."

"All according to plan," Hal replied in a dignified voice. He retrieved the flashlight, then laughed. "Hey, Jer, you've got silver zits."

After waiting for a group of students to amble past, Hal beamed his light into the hole. The bottom of the culvert glittered with thousands of bright dots. "Yes. One grate down, four to go."

In a runoff ditch near Pirate Stadium, the boys located the next grate. It was larger than the one by the student center and also welded shut. After making sure no one was in sight, Hal emptied another package.

Jerry spied grate number three in the center of a slight depression between the math building and a dorm. Ten feet away, two girls sprawled on the grass eating their lunch and studying. To distract them, Jerry pretended to be looking for his lost beagle puppy. Within two minutes, Hal completed the glitter job, and Jerry talked the girls out of a chocolate cupcake.

"Want half, Snoopy? It's your favorite doggy detective fun-food."

Hal whooped with delight. "Snoopy? Couldn't you concoct an original name?"

"How 'bout Scooby-Doo?"

Grate number four lay behind the Administrative Complex.

"We're pros at finding low places." Jerry scarfed down the cupcake.

Due to the lunch hour, the area was deserted, making the job easy.

"This one's welded shut too." Hal rolled his skateboard into a solid patch of shade.

"Wiley said they'd be."

"Right." Hal mopped his forehead with the back of his hand. "Except I'm still curious."

"Let's go eat first. Hungry beats nosey."

Hal ignored the remark. "Have you noticed the grates are different sizes?"

"Not yet."

"The ones in lower areas are larger."

"To drain more water?"

"Exactly. We need to find a grate large enough for the crooks to get bikes into the system."

Jerry plopped down beside his board. "In a deep spot."

"Secluded. The opening not welded shut."

"We've checked every low place."

"Except .... " Hal ran two fingers through his damp hair. "The location's hard to notice because it's behind a split-level building."

"The library?"

"Where else. It's built on the side of a steep hill. The front's a whole story higher than the back. I'll bet grate number five is somewhere in the general area."

Jerry scratched a mosquito bite on his leg and frowned.

"Look, we'll be fine. We haven't seen Bratton anywhere. Today's probably his day off."

Similar to the vacant building, the rear of the library bordered dense woods and had a loading platform. To Hal's disappointment, there was no sign of a drainage grate.

"Wow, look at the cool ramp." Jerry swooshed his hand in a downward motion. "What a great place to skate."

The concrete service drive didn't end at the loading platform, but turned and made a steep descent, stopping in front of a solid metal door.

"Must be an outside entrance to the basement. Let's scope it out." Hal wondered a second time if the library and vacant building were connected, both places where Bratton had a possible lead.

The boys zigzagged down the ramp. At the bottom, they found nothing except a pile of scrap lumber. The metal door, locked.

"There's no drainage grate down here." Jerry used a piece of wood to poke the pile. "Guess we'll have to copy everybody else on the planet and go eat lunch."

Hal dropped to his knees. "These thin gray lines are skid-marks." He crawled along the smooth cement. "They disappear under this pile of lumber."

"Skid-marks?"

"Only a bicycle tire makes such a narrow stripe." Hal faced his friend. "Let's get these boards out of our way."

The mound of lightweight scrap wasn't difficult to move. A steel grate twice the size of the others lay underneath.

"It's big enough to drive a food truck through." Jerry flipped aside the last piece of wood.

"Look at the latch. The weld's broken and replaced with a strong padlock." Removing the backpack from his shoulders, Hal felt the familiar tingle playing hopscotch along his spine. Finding where the crooks entered the system was no longer an issue.

The boys made short work of pouring out the last package of glitter before carefully placing the lumber back over the grate.

"Let's get outta here." Hal didn't want to alarm Jerry, but something wasn't right. The woods felt different than five minutes prior, as if dark eyes watched, while hidden ears listened.

Without warning, the metal door pushed open with an eerie creak. Both boys jumped. Bratton choked on his cigar.

"Didn't I … *cough* … tell you punks … *cough* … to keep clear of this area?" His neck veins bulged beneath wild eyes.

"Uhm, we were just, uh … taking a shortcut to the Drag for lunch. We got lost. Didn't we, Jerry."

"Don't lie to me, Tanner." Bratton took a step, barely missing the backpack. "What's in there?"

"Our dessert," Jerry squeaked. "Chocolate cupcakes. Want one?"

Bratton lunged for the backpack, then stopped cold. "Losing direction on such a big campus is easy. I'll let your confusion pass, this time."

Hal didn't know what to say. Why was Bratton letting them off?

"Thanks, Mr. Bratton, dude, um ... I mean Officer, Sir." Jerry grabbed Hal's arm. "C'mon, Hal. Let's go eat. I remember the way."

The big cop's mouth forced a molded smile. "Why don't you guys let me buy us a sandwich?"

Us?

Hal glanced in Jerry's direction.

He shrugged.

"Afterward, I'll give you a ride back to your brother's place."

"No." Hal tried to be nonchalant. "No, thanks. We've already made plans."

Bratton cleared his throat, and pronounced each syllable. "I know I acted stern with you fellows the other day. My job is protecting the general welfare by keeping citizens away from dangerous places they don't belong."

Hal offered no reply. "Come on, Jerry. Let's go."

"Listen you little—" Bratton took a deep breath, then glared at Hal. "Next time, I won't be nice."

"There won't be a next time, sir."

The plastic smile returned. "Good. Knew you'd see things my way 'cause you're a smart kid. If you change your mind about lunch, let me know. I won't be far. I'll *never* be far." He spun an about-face, strode back into the library basement, and slammed the door.

"He didn't know we were back here," Jerry whispered.

"Right. He was as surprised to see us, as we were him."

"Does he know about the grate?"

Hal hoisted his backpack. "Maybe. Makes sense why he's acting nice all of a sudden."

"One sandwich is nice? Two triple bacon cheeseburgers with fries and chocolate malt are *nice*. The guy's a cheapskate."

"I watched his eyes when he reached for the backpack. He saw something."

"The skid marks?"

"I don't know. He's scared we noticed the same thing. Figured to bleed information from us with food."

"What a dirty trick."

"Whatever the reason, we caught him sneaking around back here."

"Now he'll watch our every move." Jerry lowered his head.

Hal glanced at the scrap pile. "Let the man look. Only a mole will see us tonight. We'll be back underground."

CHAPTER ELEVEN: TRAIL OF THIEVES

The boys rushed to reach Chattanooga by eleven p.m. An hour prior, Rick appeared at the apartment to shower and grab a bite of supper. Though he complained about working late, Hal sensed excitement between his words. "Something real big's going down soon," Rick admitted as he flew out the door, offering no additional info.

Hal presumed his brother's enthusiasm centered around the mysterious caller.

Who was that person?

What did Rick know?

"Hey, look." Jerry crawled inside the azalea ring. "Wiley's put the lid back and raked dirt over it. Maybe we should forget the whole operation."

Hal set down the flashlight and began digging. "Not ... quitting ... now." He purposely separated his words. "We've come too far."

At the bottom of the ladder, they listened for echoes of footsteps or bicycle gears.

"Nothing," Hal whispered. "Let's move."

Since they weren't checking for tire tracks, the trip to the second rock room took only minutes. On a planned signal, Hal switched out the light. They advanced the last few yards in total darkness.

As soon as Hal felt the lumpy floor beneath his feet, he halted. The only sounds were the huffs of their rapid breathing. His voice trembled. "Okay, Jer, this is the correct tunnel."

"Are you sure?"

"Positive. 'Cause, we know which one *isn't* part of the main system. When I turn on the light, we'll see glitter tracked between the other two culvert openings."

"What if there isn't?"

Lord ... please. Hal flicked on the flashlight. A smattering trail of silver dots blinked back in response. "Yes," he shouted with a suppressed hiss. *Thank you.*

Jerry snapped his fingers. "Told ya."

The plan was to shine the light long enough to identify a short length of the trail, guided by memory in the darkness. Before testing another section, they'd stop and listen for sounds. If silence occupied the space, they'd repeat the same procedure.

The boys moved as swiftly as possible through the stale air. Hal kept a mental map of any side tunnels or other accessible hiding places in case of an emergency. If they had to abort the plan, they'd simply follow the glitter back to safety.

"We've passed under another grate. Makes three."

Jerry drew in his breath. "I wonder which one?"

"No clue. Size is difficult to distinguish from this angle. C'mon."

"Wait a minute." Jerry punched his watch. "Eleven-eighteen. We've been down here about twenty minutes. Why don't we take a break?"

"Too dangerous."

"I'm thirsty."

"We'll stop at the next underground rest area and buy a soft drink. Hope you brought a debit card, Jerry."

"Hilarious."

"Or maybe Wiley will bring us more ice-cold colas."

"Can't you be serious?"

"Nope. Serious ain't fun." Hal mimicked the whiney tone of his friend.

Hal's light revealed another section. Since they'd recently passed under a grate, the trail was strong. "Let's go until we reach the bend."

As they trudged forward, Hal emitted a satisfied cackle. "Reminds me of the Yellow Brick Road."

"Yeah. You're the Tin Man 'cause you don't have a heart."

"Ha-ha. You're the Scarecrow 'cause you don't have a brain."

When they reached the bend, a dot of light appeared in the distance ahead. The boys froze.

Jerry clutched the back of Hal's shirt. "I knew we shouldn't have come back. I'll never see the sixth grade."

Hal tried to recall the last side tunnel they'd passed when his reasoning kicked into overdrive. "Jerry. The dot's not moving."

"It's not?"

"Besides, the glow's from the wrong direction. The crooks are behind us. Let's go."

The tunnel slanted upward. The tiny circle of white gradually expanded into a larger square, which soon evolved into the shape of a ragged doorway.

Hal smelled the faint odor of cigarette smoke. "It's an underground room."

They crept forward, with Jerry glued to Hal's back. A large hole penetrated the culvert wall where the system made a sharp turn. Through the opening, a wide passageway was excavated and shored with lumber. The corridor led through a brick wall into what had to be the crooks' secret headquarters.

Hal's muscles quivered. "Wow. What a cool hideout. They went to great trouble."

"Okay," Jerry whispered. "We've found the bad guys. Let's get out of here and call the cops."

Hal stiffened. "We've discovered nothing but a room. I need to see the evidence."

"I appreciated your friendship more when you weren't a detective."

The boys entered the broad dugout area, littered with large cardboard boxes. Dull, shuffling sounds intermingled with the distinctive clink of metal against metal. They inched forward on tiptoes until they saw through the smashed brick wall.

Inside, a skinny bald man with tattooed arms stood beside a battery-powered camping lantern. He disassembled bicycles and stuffed them into boxes. A cigarette dangled from his thin lips.

"Yes," Hal mouthed. A wide grin connected his ears. He'd accomplished something others couldn't, including Rick.

Hal Tanner finally passed the test.

A proven winner.

The best.

A strangling grip on the neck of his T-shirt intersected Hal's revelry.

"Someone's coming." Jerry yanked on Hal's shirt again.

The echo of heavy footsteps burst into Hal's awareness as Jerry pulled him behind a large box.

"Are you trying to get us killed?" Jerry sounded more angry than scared.

As the footsteps tramped into the dugout passageway, Hal's mouth dropped in disbelief. Once again, he'd hit the top and failed. Someone else beat him to the prize.

"It's Bratton." Jerry leaned close to Hal's ear. "He must've seen the skid marks. Those crooks are gonna get caught now."

The bald man looked up from his work and scowled. "I thought I told you not to travel underground."

"Don't start with me, Yak. Got these tunnels memorized."

Hal's thoughts screamed inside his head. *Bratton's one of the thieves. Knows the system. Played down here as a kid, the same as Wiley.*

Yak lit another cigarette. His face tightened. "What your pea brain recalls don't impress me. And why aren't you watching the grate? Our friends say you're late unlocking it."

Red-faced, Bratton stepped closer to Yak. "Our *friends* also boasted how their cut of the loot will be bigger than mine."

Jerry whispered, "Is Bratton a crook, too?"

Yak sucked a long drag, then blew smoke like a dragon. "Right now, everybody gets the same. If we're caught, nobody gets nothing but trouble."

Bratton bit off part of his cigar and spit. "Any *trouble* will be the fault of those two clowns lifting bikes. A professional with my superior intellect won't make mistakes."

"Professional?" Yak horse-laughed through a smoke cloud. "You probably stole those lieutenant bars off your baby brother. He's loaded with smarts."

"You leave Wiley out of this."

The bald crook's smile oozed smug superiority. He grabbed a socket wrench and returned to his work. "Our friends report there were a couple of brats checking out your phony sign."

"Those runts don't know nothing."

Hal felt the tingle. He'd not lost after all.

Yak pointed a grease-smudged finger at Bratton. "Before you get any more brilliant ideas, check with me."

"Who made you king?" Bratton bellowed.

"You did by screwing up. Now go back, lock the grate and cover it. The men should already be underground with another load."

Bratton leaned close. "I don't have to take orders from you."

Yak blew more smoke and sneered. "Then, you won't get paid."

"I'll get my money, one way or another." Bratton straightened and stomped back into the dugout passageway. "One way or another." He slammed his cigar butt into a box near Hal and Jerry. The cop disappeared into the darkness.

Hal didn't whisper until Yak crossed to a far corner of the room. "I knew Bratton lied about the sign."

"And buying our lunch." Jerry added.

"At least we know why he wants us away from the library. But why the vacant building?"

Jerry shrugged.

"What was he looking for last night while we hid in the dumpster?"

The click of bicycle gears suspended Hal's questions. The boys scrunched lower as two backpack-clad men entered the passageway—one tall, the other short. They wore cutoffs, black sneakers, and dark T-shirts with *SSU* printed across the front.

"Hey, Yak," hollered the taller man. "Bet this baby's worth over a grand."

"Mine too," said the shorter. "There's gonna be rich kids crying in the morning."

The two crooks snickered.

"Park those bikes and shut up," Yak demanded from across the room. "Did you see Bratton?"

"Yeah, we passed him." The shorter one parked his bike. "The big ape's harsh words stung our delicate ears. What's his problem?"

"Maybe he smells himself." The taller one mimed sniffing his armpit.

Both men snickered louder.

Yak moved back into Hal's view. "Bratton's work is sloppy and will blow our profits. He needs to disappear."

THE GLITTER EFFECT

Whaaah. Whaaah. Whaaah.

Hal scrambled to mute the alarm signaling Jerry's next snack.

Caught.

CHAPTER TWELVE: TALKIN' TRASH

"Get 'em," Yak shouted.

The two men grabbed Hal and Jerry, dragging them into the lighted room.

"How special. We have visitors." Yak lit another cigarette. "Perhaps our guests prefer to sit?"

The men pushed the boys onto the hard floor.

"Ouch." Jerry cried. "That hurt."

"Hey, Harvey. Better be easy 'cause he'll tattle to his mama," sing-songed the shorter man.

Harvey's grin split his leathery face. "Didn't she teach him not to spy on upstanding citizens?"

"Tsk, tsk." The shorter man wiggled his finger. "Snooping into the private business of others is naughty."

The men shook with laughter.

"Shut up," Yak growled. "Plug, run check this end of the tunnel and see if anybody else is sneaking around."

The shorter man darted out of the room. The muscles in his arms and legs equaled those of an Olympic weight lifter.

"You'd better let us go." Hal rose to his knees.

"Hey, boss? The thin one's got guts. Let's keep him and throw back the thick one."

"Tie 'em up." Yak pitched Harvey a roll of gray duct tape. "I'll keep an eye on the tunnel."

Jerry sat in a daze. From the moment the watch alarm sounded, he'd barely moved a muscle. He didn't bother to wipe the occasional tear on his cheek.

Harvey jerked Hal's hands behind his back, bound his wrists, and taped his feet together. He repeated the same procedure on Jerry.

"What now, boss?"

Yak paced back and forth, cursing under his breath. Every few seconds, he'd glare at Hal and Jerry.

Plug shot back into the room. "Tunnel's clean."

Yak stopped pacing. A blanket of hate covered his face. "Because of Mister Bratton's foolish mistakes, I have no choice but to shut down the entire operation."

"Boss?"

"He let a couple of punk kids find us. You wanna go back to jail?"

"Not me." Plug raised his hands in surrender and shook his head.

Harvey raised his hands too.

"We'll ride out with the midnight shipment. You two start hauling boxes upstairs. Put *everything* inside the dumpsters. I don't want a single fingerprint left behind.

Upstairs?

Dumpsters?

The words slapped Hal in the face.

Cardboard boxes.

Duct tape.

Yes.

For the first time, the odd puzzle pieces fit.

He glanced at Jerry.

No response.

Was his friend aware the underground room was the basement of the vacant classroom building? The place where bikes were disassembled, before smuggled off campus in garbage trucks?

Yak hacked a throaty laugh. "Bratton still won't get nothing. By the time he inspects the dumpster area, we'll be long gone."

Plug and Harvey bumped fists.

"Get to work," Yak picked up his tools. "We don't have much time."

"What about the kids?" Plug scratched his head.

Yak sucked a final drag, dropped the butt, and ground it with his shoe. His eyes bore an evil gleam. "Stuff the brats in a box. We'll dispose of 'em with the rest of the trash."

"No way," Hal shouted. "You're not putting us anywhere."

"Shut the shrimp up." Yak turned back to clearing his worktable.

Plug grabbed the duct tape and headed toward the boys. Hal rocked back, cocked his feet, and kicked Plug in the stomach with both barrels. The stocky crook doubled over, gasping for air.

"Why you little—" Harvey seized a large screwdriver and rushed toward Hal.

"No-o-o." Jerry nudged a set of handlebars into Harvey's path, tripping him into a stack of loaded boxes.

Yak exploded. "Can't you ladies do nothin' right? Now drop the screwdriver and finish the job neat. I don't want cops finding blood."

Plug secured each boy in a bear-hug while Harvey smashed duct tape over their mouths.

Yak faced the passageway and pointed to a large box. "Put 'em in there and seal it tight."

Pushed inside feet first, Jerry offered little resistance.

Hal squirmed and fought, finally forced inside on his head. The crooks secured the lid. Both boys lay on their sides back to back, heads at opposite ends, hostages in total darkness.

Hal tried to move, though there was little room. A foul odor made him gag. At first, he thought it was Jerry's sneakers, then realized the smell originated from something slimy and cold pressing his cheek. Hal wiggled his head in an attempt to scoot the object away from his face. The action only repositioned it, worsening the stench.

And, then he remembered.

When Bratton stormed out of the underground room, he'd thrown something into a box. A few minutes later, Yak chose the same box to imprison the boys. Lodged against Hal's mouth and nose was the cop's spit-oozing cigar butt.

Time crept to a mind numbing halt.

Hal trembled.

Cold drops of sweat trickled down his face. His left eye stung, but he couldn't wipe it. He heard the muted whiz of socket wrenches, the scratch of cardboard dragged across the gritty floor.

Occasional laughter was followed by the strained bark of additional orders.

Hal felt light-headed. Yak's orders smothered his thoughts. He and Jerry would be hauled somewhere and dumped like garbage.

Then what?

The gag, plus the cigar butt made breathing difficult. Perhaps if he could inch his sneakers against the taped end of the box, he could kick it open when the crooks left the room. He wormed his way down until the tape binding his wrists snagged on Jerry's watch and halted his progress.

Stupid watch.

Hot tears stung his other eye. Tears of anger. He wished he could smash Jerry's watch into a million pieces. Why was Hal best friends with a guy who was forever hungry? And why would anyone—including Jerry—want to hang out with a chronic loser?

Help us, Lord. Please free us from this box.

Images of Jonah imprisoned inside the whale's belly washed through Hal's mind. The man must have been terrified.

Yet God remained with him.

Taught him.

Strengthened him.

I know you're with us, Heavenly father. Use me. Teach me what you want me to know.

Hurried footsteps laced with heated cries burst into the room. "Don't let him get away," shouted a gruff tone.

Bratton?

"You dirty double-crosser." Yak tacked on a string of obscenities. "You'll pay for this."

Hal heard more footsteps, followed by a loud crash of bicycle parts. A man's voice he didn't recognize commanded Yak handcuffed and hauled upstairs. "Take him outside with the other two perpetrators and read 'em their rights."

Yak continued his protest. "Hey? Bratton was in on the deal too, from the beginning. I swear he knew all about it."

"He's a stinking liar." Bratton's voice was deep and hard.

"No one jerks me around," Yak shouted. "You're a dead man, Curtis Bratton."

The threats faded as the back-slapping began. Someone related how Yak—a local ex-con with a history of thefts—hated cops and threatened to destroy law enforcement.

Others shared similar stories.

Words congratulating Bratton's great detective work filled the room, mingled with shouts of a promotion. Someone familiar asked questions.

Rick.

The electric tingle resumed, vibrating Hal's spine, echoing truth. Bratton presumed the crooks would cheat him, thus disguised his voice and tipped off the press. He'd get the reward money *and* a promotion—the perfect plan. If the crooks accused the cop, he'd deny everything. No one believed a bunch of thieves caught in the act. And what officer risked squealing on himself?

A trio of thoughts hurt Hal's heart:

One: Bratton pulled off the lie of the century.

Two: He'd be crowned a hero.

Three: Rick would write a winning story.

"Not fair," Hal screamed into the sticky gag. "Not to Wiley."

Oh Lord ... I don't care about the reward money anymore, or becoming the best skater. I want everyone to know Wiley is the real hero.

Excitement over the arrest ricocheted around the room. Bratton boasted how he'd solved the case. The man who'd sent Yak upstairs spoke of a promotion. Rick addressed the man as Chief Nelson.

Hal kicked and screamed, but no one heard over the celebration. Out of desperation, Hal again tried sliding to the end of the box. If only he could free his wrists from Jerry's watch.

Jerry's watch.

Hal strained. The strong tape cut into his flesh. He managed to get a thumb and forefinger positioned across the bottom edge of the watch's face. He pushed a button.

Nothing.

He stretched for another button.

His fingers slipped.

The hubbub subsided.

Rick asked more questions.

Time was running out.

Pushing harder, Hal forced the tape into a death grip around his wrists.

This time, Jerry understood and pressed the watch closer within Hal's grasp.

Hal punched two more buttons.

No sound.

THE GLITTER EFFECT

The chance of rescue faded fast. Days could pass before anyone found them, or the crooks decided to tell—which was too late.

Rick stopped talking.

The voices are leaving.

With all the strength Hal could muster, he reached for what he hoped was the red panic button. His finger missed, but the nail hit its mark.

Whaaah. Whaaah. Whaaah.

CHAPTER THIRTEEN: ALL THAT GLITTERS

The ripping of cardboard was music to Hal's squashed ears. When his eyes focused, he witnessed astonishment on each officer's face.

Bratton's most of all.

"Hal? Jerry? What are you—? How did you—?" Rick's questions slammed to a stop.

Hal screamed into his gag, making frantic head motions toward Bratton.

"Cut them loose." Chief Nelson ordered.

The officer peeled the duct tape from the boys' mouths.

"Bratton's a crook." Hal struggled to stand up. "I can prove it."

The big cop's eyes narrowed. "Kid's trying to get me back 'cause I scolded him." Bratton's bravado wavered. "Children have no understanding of complicated police work."

Hal wiped his sticky mouth on his shirt sleeve. "Officer Bratton was down here earlier tonight. He argued with Yak. Jerry and I hid in the tunnel. We heard everything."

"It's the truth," Jerry added.

Bratton's face glowed like hot coals. "I don't have to listen to fairy tales."

"You guys were in the drainage tunnels?" Rick slapped his forehead in disbelief.

Chief Nelson made a circular motion with his index finger. Two officers blocked Bratton's way. "Now son, tell me what you know."

Hal repeated what transpired between Bratton and Yak. The heated talk about money and the grate behind the library.

"He's lying." Bratton tried to shoulder past the officers. "I don't know anything about a grate, nor stepped inside this room until tonight."

"What about this?" Hal grabbed the chewed cigar butt. "I saw him throw it into the box before he left through the tunnel."

Sweat poured down Bratton's face. "Don't prove nothing. Could belong to anybody." He glanced at the chief. "Kid's crazy. I wouldn't set foot in the old underground drainage system. It's way too dangerous."

"Look at his shoes, Chief." Hal nudged Jerry. "I'll bet there's silver glitter on the soles."

"Glitter?" Bratton sneered. "And there are paints in my pockets and crayons under my shirt."

Chief Nelson crossed his arms. "Let the boy speak."

Hal told about *The Glitter Effect*, and how they'd followed the shiny trail to the crooks.

Rick beamed. "I'm impressed."

"Go stand by the lantern and remove your shoes." Chief Nelson cocked his head toward the table.

"This ain't no kindergarten art class. I don't have to do—"

"That's an order. If you're innocent, you've nothing to fear."

Scowling, Bratton stomped to the light.

"Take 'em off slowly." Chief Nelson stepped toward him. "We don't want to miss anything."

Bratton cursed under his breath and bent over. He reached for his right shoe. Instead, he grabbed a wrench and smashed the lantern.

Darkness and confusion followed before flashlights pierced the blackness.

"He's run into the tunnel," someone shouted.

From the dug-out passageway came a dull thud, followed by a loud moan.

"There he is," came another shout. "Bratton's down."

Flashlight beams bobbed from inside of the passageway. "Cuff him," Chief Nelson barked. "Good thing he fell or we might've lost him. Guess he tripped over his own two feet."

Someone switched on another lantern. Two officers escorted Bratton back through the underground room, then out the door. His face wore a silent, blank expression.

Chief Nelson grinned. "You boys have a healthy reward coming."

"Plus a front-page story." Rick's pride neared the bursting point.

Hal and Jerry slapped hands.

"Although, there's still a mystery." Rick stroked his chin. "How did you guys get into the drainage system? It was sealed years ago."

An officer stepped into the room. "We need you up top, sir."

"We'd better go." Chief Nelson gestured behind Hal. "Is that yours?"

The big flashlight.

Hal had forgotten all about it, dropped in the passageway when Plug and Harvey grabbed them. Who'd placed the light in the underground room?

Instantly, Hal knew.

The same person who'd tripped Bratton in the dugout passageway. Alongside were two colas ... ice-cold.

"The flashlight belongs to us both." Hal breathed a heavy sigh of relief and laughed out loud.

The next morning, Rick printed a special edition featuring the capture and arrest of the bicycle theft ring. A picture of Hal and Jerry accepting a one-thousand-dollar reward check adorned the front page, along with details on how they'd solved the crime.

There were also mug shots of the crooks—more than willing to rat on each other. Yak was a former SSU electrician who'd served time for stealing power tools. While in jail, he met Plug and Harvey, who'd helped plot the underground bike heist. Upon release, they chose Bratton to run the topside cover-up. The garbage truck driver was Yak's friend.

Hal and Jerry sat inside Rick's office. He read the article aloud for the third time, leaned back, and propped both feet on his desk. "I'll bet Mom and Dad will demand copies for all the relatives."

"Cool." Jerry's head nodded like a bobble doll.

Hal blushed. Maybe they'd frame a copy and hang it in the den.

"So what are you guys going to do with the reward money? Start a private detective agency?"

"Maybe." Hal grinned. "We'll save most of it."

"Unless we spend half on pizza," Jerry added.

Everyone laughed.

Whaaah. Whaaah. Whaaah.

"Uh-oh." Rick recrossed his feet. "Must be time to feed the baby. I owe you guys lunch."

"Sorry." Hal put his hands on his chair arms. "We're meeting someone."

"At Jolly Roger's?"

"No." Jerry scooted to the edge of his seat. "Chattanooga."

Rick scrunched his nose. "Tennessee?"

Hal and Jerry stood.

"Gotta pay back a guy." Hal turned to leave.

The boys scampered out the door.

"Pay someone back?" Rick's feet slammed to the floor. "Wait a minute. How much do you owe?"

"Everything," Hal shouted. "We owe him everything. Plus a bunch of colas—ice-cold."

THE END

ABOUT THE AUTHOR

Timothy Lewis is author of the bestselling novel, *Forever Friday*, which was translated into multiple languages and featured in *Reader's Digest Select Editions*. He's only the second *Reader's Digest* author of an inspirational crossover title in over twenty-five years. Reviewers on BookBub, Goodreads, Barnes & Noble, and Amazon compared his poetic prose to Nicholas Sparks. In an article for *USA Today*, a literary editor likened Tim to Garrison Keillor.

As a published playwright, Tim's penned more than twenty plays/musicals and over a hundred songs. His article, *Freighting on the XIT Ranch of Texas*, was published in the *Panhandle-Plains Historical Review*. Committed to help fellow writers, he cofounded the West Texas Writers' Academy, held annually at West Texas A&M University.

Mr. Lewis holds a bachelor's degree of Music Education (BMED) from Sam Houston State University, and studied master's level playwrighting at The University of Texas.

Moreover, he's a graduate of The Institute of Children's Literature and a cowboy poet.

Tim and his wife, Dinah, live "happily ever after" atop the beautiful high plains of Texas.

If you've enjoyed *The Glitter Effect*, Tim would appreciate you writing a short review and posting on Amazon, Goodreads, and/or Barnes & Noble. To contact Tim, check his website,

Made in the USA
Columbia, SC
12 November 2021